I0598165

Family Secrets

Book 2

Augusta Wright

© 2018 Augusta Wright
All rights reserved.

ISBN: 0998296716
ISBN 13: 9780998296715

A talebearer revealeth secrets,
But he that is a faithful spirit concealeth the matter.

Proverbs 11:13 (KJV)

1

May 1889, Spotted Horse Ranch, Colorado Rockies

WILL

Loud, drunken snores filled the early-morning quiet as the sky lightened. Slobber streamed down the spotted horse's neck and pooled at its left hoof as its rider hung precariously spread-eagle on its back.

Indian Blanket, one of the great-grandsons of Spotted Horse, Eagle Talon's stallion, pawed the ground to show his impatience as he waited for Will to get down.

The rider did not move.

When the stallion violently shook itself, the motion caused the rider to slide from its back, and he hit the hard ground like a sack of potatoes. The stallion nickered as it looked around at its rider, who was now lying prone on the ground. Getting no response, it turned and trotted toward its warm stall in the barn.

Shallow gasps followed as Will attempted to draw air back into his depleted lungs.

When he was able to breathe, he came out of his drunken fog long enough to stare up through the tall pines at the fingers of light brightening the dark sky above him. He tried to remember if his horse had thrown him or if he had fallen off. He didn't even know where he was.

Still trying to get a clearer idea of where he was, he managed to push himself up to a sitting position, and then he recognized the front yard of his mother's cabin. He shook his fist at the rump of the vanishing horse as he yelled, "Damn smart-ass horse. Who do you think you are, bringing me here?"

With exasperated sighs, he struggled to get his feet under himself but succeeded only in getting on all fours as he crawled up the two steps to the wooden plank porch.

Before reality rushed into his whiskey-filled brain, he cried out, "Mother, it's me. Don't shoot!"

But as soon as the words were uttered, he knew there would be no answer from within. His mother was dead. His body sagged, and his lips quivered as the immense sadness flowed over him.

He stared at the faded claw marks that still marred the door to her cabin. A bear had made them long ago as it tried to get in. His memories echoed with her voice telling the exciting tale of how she had survived.

After inching his way to the door, he pushed it open as he pulled himself upright, using the doorframe as a brace.

He made a good attempt to stand but staggered this way and that before he fell in front of the cold fireplace on his mother's prized bearskin rug, where he drew himself into a fetal position and cried like a baby for his mother.

Will Ralston Brown had continued to slide into a great despair since his mother's sudden death last year. At first, he had tried to ignore the fact that she was gone. And any help from his siblings and friends was rejected. He had worked himself to exhaustion so he would not have to deal with her death. But that didn't help, either.

Now he turned to whiskey. Aha, whiskey! It was the answer for anyone wanting to numb the brain. Will anticipated that it would not let him think or feel. He had hoped it would keep him from any thoughts of her or anything else, for that matter. That was the solace he had been seeking, but whiskey wasn't working, either. He was drunk again—and there was still no relief from his agony. He passed out as large tears streamed down his handsome face.

Later in the day, he managed to open one eye and then the other as he tried to remember where he was. His bloodshot eyes searched the room, and he was surprised when he saw he was in his mother's cabin.

How did I get here? When did I get here?

For some strange reason, he felt relief, something he had not felt since Mother had passed. Could it be her spirit soothing his troubled soul? He wished she would soothe his pounding head with one of her special teas.

He managed to crawl to her rocking chair and pulled himself up to sit in it. Dizziness overwhelmed him, but he fought to stay in the chair. He leaned his head back and closed his eyes. He liked the feel of her chair; it was as if her arms were around him, rocking him as she used to when he was younger and unhappy or hurt. He rocked for some time before he decided he needed coffee.

Slowly rising, bracing himself, he swayed and staggered to her old wood cookstove. He managed to get a fire going, found the coffee, and discovered water still in the old barrel by the door. Before long, he had a cup of strong coffee in his shaky hands and was back sitting in her chair. He looked around the cabin she had loved so dearly.

He wondered why.

Her early life here had been hard and lonely. She had told them stories about when his father had died, leaving her alone to struggle and survive before he and his twin brother, Eli, were born.

Mother had struggled but managed to provide for them, and Will was proud of her for it. She had saved her family, but still he did not know much about that time in her early years here, and he realized with deep sorrow he would never know.

Why hadn't he ever asked her questions? He was so stupid. He thought he would always have her here with him. He had depended upon her more than he'd ever known until she was suddenly gone. He knew she was smart in book knowledge but also in plain old horse sense. If people had horse sense, "they were smart," she always told him.

He wondered if any of her horse sense had been passed on to him. He had his doubts, especially about the way he had been behaving since her death. He did have her special ability to communicate with animals. They responded to her, and she knew what they needed or how to care for them. It had pleased her when she'd found out her special gift had been passed to him.

She'd helped him understand how special his gift with horses and wild animals was. It was something they'd shared. His mother had been amazing in so many ways.

For the first time, Will thought about her special friend, Silver, with the blue eyes. The wolf had been her constant companion whenever she was out working. He had not seen the wolf since Mother had died. Why had he disappeared? Where was he now?

He spilled his hot coffee on his shirt as he jerked his fist up at her painting on the mantle and yelled out in his hurt and anger, "Why didn't you tell me you were sick? Why did you leave me all alone? Why, Mother? Didn't you know I needed you? I am all alone now."

Unshed tears welled up in his eyes as he looked at her in the painting. When they overflowed, the tears splashed down his tan cheeks, wetting his shirt as they dripped off his jaws. He vented his frustration and grief on the silent cabin.

After some time, he recovered and resumed his rocking. He did feel better. He was not sure if it was from the coffee or his venting. Maybe both. His eyes continued to move about the room as if searching for something that would help him through his deep grief and loss.

At last, his eyes touched on her Bible sitting on the small table between the two rocking chairs. Her eyeglasses lay on top of it as if she had just finished reading and gone outside. With shaking hands, he picked up her glasses and looked at them. He could see smudges on the lenses, perhaps smudges she had made the last time she used them.

He sniffled loudly, wiping his runny nose on his sleeve.

He picked up her well-worn Bible and held it reverently to his nose as if to catch a scent of her essence from the bindings. She had taught her children to read and follow the teachings of Jesus from this Bible. It hit him like a pine tree falling on him that he had moved away from the teachings since her death. He had become lost in his grief for her.

Clutching the Bible to his chest, he cried hard for his mother and for his pain at her loss. His grief was so commanding his body shook with his sobs.

A comforting presence flowed into the room and settled over him. Peace spread through him, a feeling he had not had since her death. His emptiness was being filled.

"Mother, are you here with me?" He sensed her loving spirit surrounding him. What a blessed relief he felt.

He prayed for forgiveness and help overcoming his deep grief as his mother had taught him to pray. As he leaned his head back into her chair, he felt her love all around him. He slipped into a restful sleep as he still hugged her Bible. He slept the sleep of someone who had the weight of the world lifted off his shoulders.

His soul was comforted. His grief had lessened. Mother was here.

Hours later he awoke again. Shadows danced on the walls, as the day had passed, and it was growing darker. He rubbed his neck to work the crick out, but he felt peace in his heart for the first time in a year. Looking at the Bible still in his hands, he opened it.

In different sections of Laura's Bible were four sealed envelopes addressed to each of her children. His was marked "Will—my firstborn" and inserted at Psalm 23, his favorite scripture. His letter had been there all the time. All he'd had to do was look for it. He should have known his mother would not leave him without a word. He laughed aloud because his mother always had the last word, and here it was.

He gently opened the envelope and removed the letter. It began:

> My Dearest Will,
>   You were always my favorite, even though I tried not to show favoritism for you in front of your siblings. You

were the most handsome and always so much smarter than your brothers and your sister. But please don't tell them. It would only hurt them.

If you are reading this, then I have already gone. There was so much I wanted to say to you before but could not. I have kept journals of my life here on the frontier so you, your siblings, and my grandchildren would know how we lived and who we were. I have numbered each in the order I want you to read them. I pray you will understand some of the decisions I made and why.

Some were made with my heart, some were made in fear, but all were made to keep my family safe. There may be parts that will make you angry or ashamed of me, and I pray you will forgive me. I am only human and have the same desires and needs as you. You will not understand until you read the journals. Perhaps afterward, you will understand me on a different level, and you will understand yourself as well.

You will find the journals behind an Indian basket in a safe hidden in the cellar for safekeeping important papers and money if we had any. The combination is at the bottom of this page.

These journals tell the story of my life. After you have read them, please replace them in the safe so your siblings will know where to find them. I will always be with you and love you.

Your loving mother,
Laura Ralston Brown
Spirit Woman of the Ute Warrior Eagle Talon

Will's hands shook as he reread the letter several times, seeking consolation from her handwritten words to him. He smiled in places where she stoked his ego and frowned in others when he did not fully understand her meanings. He would not understand until he read her journals. He'd never known she kept them. It hurt to know she had kept secrets from him, but then he realized reading her journals would reveal all her secrets. Was he prepared to do that?

He wondered.

He needed food before he could continue. He sat motionless for a while as a plan formed in his mind. First, he had to sober up. He had to eat and be ready for anything that came out of the journals at him. He would bring food here and lock himself in until he had completed his task, no matter how long it took.

Only then would he share all the letters with his siblings. He knew it was selfish, but he was not ready for them to know about the letters. It was obvious they had not come seeking Mother, either. He was the firstborn. He would be first in this also!

2

Matt Wilson

Matt Wilson, the ranch foreman, heard the approaching horse and wondered who was riding up this early in the morning. Looking down from the hayloft, he was surprised to see Will's stallion, Indian Blanket, coming in without Will.

He heard Marty talking to the horse before he looked down from the hayloft to see her catch him near the barn. He saw movement at the front of Laura's cabin and realized it was Will crawling on all fours.

Drunk again! Would that boy ever learn?

But as soon as he thought it, he knew the great sorrow her death had caused. Matt had loved Laura from the moment he met her when he was a young boy. She was the most beautiful woman he had ever seen, with the kindest heart. She saved his family in their darkest hours and bought the homestead from Mother so she could return to her family in the South after a bear killed Father. She was an angel who had been sent to his family in their hour of need.

She had confided in him her deeply guarded secret that her husband was dead, not wanting anyone to know except him. He had kept the secret even now. He never wanted any shame to fall on her because he knew the twins had been born too long after her husband died. His love for her drew him to return to her with the promise of a job on her ranch. He came with his wife, whom he loved very much. But Laura was his first love, and he would do anything for her.

Since she had passed, he had entertained ideas of moving his family to Texas to buy land. He'd always wanted to own his own land like his father had. He'd heard stories of land there for the taking. He had saved his wages and had a good nest egg.

"Humph," he grunted softly as he threw another pitchfork full of hay into the fodder box below. He liked the idea more and more. These winters here were just too damn cold for his bones.

3

Will

Will had his twin, Eli, to deal with right now. His twin! That had always sounded funny, since they did not look anything alike. Will was more than six feet tall, lean, dark tan skin and black, wavy hair. His cobalt blue eyes were like Mother's.

His twin, Eli, was shorter with a stockier, more muscular build, green eyes, fair skin, and reddish-blond hair.

The only things that made them twins were that they had the same parents and were born within two minutes of each other. They were always in competition for their parents' attention. They fought about everything. They were brothers, but something was missing in their understanding of each other.

Since Mother had passed, Black Hawk, their brother who was a year younger, had stayed with his Ute Indian family more than with them. His grandmother, Running Fawn, was teaching him more of tribal medicine as he became a shaman like his father, Eagle Talon.

Black Hawk had always been more Indian than Will and Eli. When he began having visions when he was young, Eagle Talon had been a strong force in teaching Black Hawk about becoming a shaman. However, Father had been wise in not pressuring him to choose which world to live in. He wanted him to make the right choice for himself.

It was obvious Black Hawk's fine looks would allow him to pass in either world. He was taller and more heavily muscled than his Indian cousins. His hair was black, but his skin tones were a sun-darkened brown like his Indian father, who exhibited features from his French father. But the dark-blue eyes were definitely from Mother.

Now he also was awash in his grief, and no one knew how to deal with the loss.

Their younger sister, Raven, who was now eighteen, had grown into a beautiful woman. She was tall for a Ute maiden. Her long black hair fell in ringlets down her back when she did not have it braided. Her looks were different from Black Hawk's. Her skin had a dusky hue, showing her grandfather's European breeding, but Mother's fairness lightened it. Her most outstanding feature was her blue eyes that sparkled like sapphires when she smiled.

But she was not here with them. She had been sent to their mother's younger sister, Jane, who lived in Washington. Auntie Jane was to teach Raven about being a lady. They always saw her in pants, racing bareback on one of the spotted stallions as she yelled like a wild Indian on a raid—which was very unladylike.

Their parents had been unable to control her, no matter how much they tried. No amount of teaching and punishing completely bought her under control.

Mother had wanted her to learn to run a home, garden, preserve food, and read Bible verses for her to become a chaste woman. She wanted her to marry well.

Their father had wanted Raven to learn the ways of his People by living with them, so when the time came, she would be able to choose a mate from his world or her mother's world.

Raven would have none of it.

Raven had been gone now for over two years. Mother had gotten weekly letters from Auntie Jane about her progress, which had been very slow because she continued to rebel. However, after Mother died, the letters came sparingly. They had not heard from Raven at all.

Will had sat contemplating the many problems with his siblings. But how to fix them? He did not know. When he rose and opened the cabin door to return to the big house, he was startled to see Silver, his mother's white wolf, sitting near the bench Mother loved to sit on. His sky-blue eyes stared into Will's sad, dark ones before Silver turned and trotted back into the forest.

Will was stunned to see Silver. No one had seen him since the day Mother died. A shiver ran up and down his spine as he thought about what the meaning of it could be. Was he imagining the wolf? Or was it a sign from Mother that all would be well again?

Shaking himself, he walked to the big house, deciding what he would say to convince everyone to stay away from the cabin. He wanted to be alone with his thoughts. That sounded good. It seemed to make sense because they were worried about him and his sullenness and heavy drinking.

At the evening meal with Eli, he made the announcement about his plans to spend a few days in Mother's cabin.

"What do you mean, Will? What has come over you?" asked Eli in disbelief.

"I realized this morning when I woke up from another drunken stupor in Mother's cabin that I couldn't continue the way I was going. I didn't want to let myself grieve for her and tried my best not to. But I know now I have to let it in."

"You think staying in her cabin will make a difference?"

"Yes, I do. I will start tomorrow morning with help from you and Sadie. I need food, fresh water, and wood. When I come out, I pray I will be a better man."

"OK, Will. I'll help you any way I can."

The next morning, Sadie Long, their housekeeper, cook, and long-time friend, packed a large basket with fresh-ground coffee, a loaf of homemade bread, fried chicken, breakfast fixings, and of course, his favorite cookies.

Eli replenished the water barrel and wood supply before he left him at the door.

Waving goodbye, Will began his journey into his mother's life. He went inside the cabin and barred the heavy door.

Then he began.

4

Will

The morning of the third day, Will opened the cabin door and walked out on the porch. He looked around, seeing everything in a different way than when he'd gone into the cabin.

Everything had changed.

He had changed.

He wondered if his mother had known how her journals would affect him. How they would change the family. They had made him laugh, cry, and experience passion and extreme anger. He was changed, but for the first time, he understood how this ranch had changed his mother from a silly little girl into the strong woman of the West that he knew.

This land was harsh and uncaring. If you did not prepare, it killed you. His mother had learned early what had to be done, and she did it. He could not fault her for anything. She had made choices to protect herself and her family. One of her sayings popped into his head: "Sometimes you have to bargain with the devil and pray to the Lord you win."

Now he understood what she had referred to.

He had the answer to why his brother Eli and he were so dissimilar. They had different fathers! Strange how that had happened. Well, not strange but certainly unusual. He had never thought of a threesome before.

When he had visited the saloon girls, he had had only one at a time. When his mother found out, however, he quickly learned why he should keep it buttoned in his pants. After she finished telling him and showing a medical book with pictures of cocks rotting off from diseases picked up in whorehouses, he had quickly lost his taste for loose women.

With all his drunkenness of late, he still did not go upstairs at the saloon. He played cards and drank with his friends. But he did have a special, lonely widow lady on a small ranch not too far from here he visited from time to time. She had taught him many things about loving he never wanted his mother to know he knew.

He laughed out loud. After reading her journals, she probably could have taught him some new tricks. He quickly blanked out those thoughts because he did not want to think of his mother doing any of those activities! She was Mother.

Now that he knew the truth, he felt better. She had kept the letters from the two men with their names, information about their families, and where they were going. She had written each man a letter dated a few days before she died. He had seen his full name and his siblings' names in his mother's Bible. It had all become clearer. He had always sensed Abner Brown was not his father. Why? Perhaps Mother's way of talking about his father was different from the way she spoke of Abner Brown.

Will knew Eagle Talon was not. They did not have the same features or even resemble each other. Eli certainly did not look like him, either. But Talon had loved both boys as if they were his own flesh and blood. He was a wonderful father. Will was glad to have had him in their lives, and Eagle Talon had loved their mother.

Love was important. He wondered if he would ever fall in love and have someone special in his life to care for as his mother had.

He heard a shout from the barn as Eli saw him on the porch. He waved and set off for the barn. When they met, Will gave Eli a bear hug, which surprised his brother.

"Are you all right?" he asked with concern and surprise on his face.

"I am better than I have been in a very long time, little brother," he answered using an endearing term he had not used since they were little.

Eli's stunned look said it all.

"I wonder what Sadie has for supper. I am starving," Will said as he headed toward the big house.

"Are you going to tell me anything about what has been going on?" Eli yelled as he ran to catch up.

"Nope, not till after supper," he said as he continued to walk fast.

Will bathed, shaved, and dressed in a clean shirt and pants before he came downstairs to eat supper with Eli. Sadie had outdone herself in preparing fried steak, mashed potatoes, gravy, large biscuits, and fresh vegetables from the early spring garden.

After the meal, which was eaten with the usual conversation of ranch business and new spotted foals, Will and Eli sat finishing their desserts and coffee.

Finally, Will said, "As you well know, I have had a very difficult time accepting Mother's unexpected death. I tried to ignore what had happened in various ways, including using alcohol. And nothing worked until I ended up in Mother's cabin. That has truly been my turning point. Have you grieved for her yet?" he asked his brother pointedly.

Eli dropped his head, nodding. "I have tried to move on, but I have had no one to help me. You did not want to share with me, and I have just held it in." His voice quivered as he said this.

"Well, little brother, I will help you. I want you to spend time as I did in Mother's cabin, and you will emerge a new man. I promise. Will you agree to do what I ask?" He stared at Eli across the table.

"I am at a place where I will agree to anything. I feel so alone. My family is no longer here, and I do not know what to do. We seem to have lost our way, Will," replied Eli affectionately.

"Tomorrow we will get you set up in Mother's cabin, and when you come out, we will sit down and talk about everything you learned. And trust me, it is going to be a learning experience," he told his brother excitedly.

5

Eli

After breakfast the next morning, Will carried another large basket of foodstuffs Sadie had prepared for Eli and his sojourn in Mother's cabin.

"As I sat there in the cabin thinking of our mother, I noticed her Bible. When I picked it up, I discovered she had left each one of us a letter placed in various chapters of her Bible. Mine was in Psalm 23. Yours is in I Corinthians 13. I think she chose comforting chapters for each of us. Anyway, little brother, you must read her letter to you and do what it tells you to do. When you come out, we will have much to talk about." Will said this as he hugged Eli before he turned, closed the cabin door behind him, and left Eli standing in the middle of the cabin.

Eli found the letter in Mother's Bible where Will had said. He opened it gently and reverently. She wrote:

> My Dearest Eli:
> You were always my favorite, even though I tried not to show favoritism for you in front of your siblings. You

were the most handsome and always so much smarter than your brothers and your sister. But please don't tell them. It would only hurt them.

If you are reading this, then I have already gone. There was so much I wanted to say to you before but could not. I kept a journal of our lives here on the frontier so you, your siblings, and my grandchildren would know how we lived and who we were...

The letter continued as the first one had, explaining where the journals could be found.

Three days later, a blurry-eyed, unshaven, and unwashed Eli walked out on the front porch of his mother's cabin. He felt at peace on some level, but with the knowledge he now had, he felt uncertain of what to do. His world as he knew it had certainly changed. He prayed it would be for the good. Right now, he was very confused about what he knew about his mother's past and what he knew about himself.

Will had been sitting on the front porch of the ranch house waiting for Eli to emerge. He could see, even from that distance, Eli's uncertainty, which showed in his body language. He waited for him to see him and signal for him to come to the cabin. He was anxious to talk with someone about what he knew.

Finally, Eli saw him and waved. Will shot off the porch and hurried up to the Widow's Peak, where Eli was now standing, looking out over the valley.

"I always get a peaceful feeling when I come up here and look out over the river valley. I know why Mother loved this place," Eli said as he sat down on the bench where their mother liked to sit. He felt his shaky legs would not hold him much longer.

"Are you all right, Eli?" Will asked with concern in his voice as he looked at his brother's ashen face and placed a hand on Eli's shoulder.

"I am still reeling from what I have read. I have so many questions, and I truly do not know what to do with the knowledge I now have. My family as I knew it is not the family I thought it was," Eli said with a quivering voice.

Will sat down by his brother as he said, "But that is not true. We are still brothers, but we now understand why we are so different. I had many questions rolling around in my mind for years, which were answered by discovering we have different fathers. Remember, we do have the same mother and are of the same blood. You are still my twin brother, and do not ever forget it. Do you understand me?" He raised his voice to make his point.

Eli could not speak, for emotion had risen in his throat as he hugged his brother to him. At that point, neither one was able to speak. Softly Eli asked, "Did you sense Mother in there with you?"

"Yes, Eli, she was there and always has been. We only needed to seek her out. Didn't it make you feel better?"

He croaked out, "Yes, and I needed reassurance we still had each other. Thank you for loving me even though we are so different."

"We are different, but we are so much alike, too," Will said. "We both came from our mother's body, and we have many traits from her. But we have many traits from our fathers as well."

"We will have to learn about ourselves as we work to put this family back together to survive. Do you understand what I am trying to say?" Will asked Eli as they looked at each other.

Eli nodded and asked, "But what do we do first?"

"You look like hell. Have you eaten anything?" Will asked with concern in his voice.

"No. But I want us to go back inside and talk about what we have found out. I am still trying to wrap my mind around some things you may be able to help me with," Eli said as he looked hopefully at his brother.

"Good idea. I will fix you some breakfast while we discuss these revelations and what our next step should be," he said as he pulled Eli up on his feet and headed him in the direction of their mother's cabin.

6

The Twins

When the twins next emerged from the cabin, it was late in the evening. They had reread parts of their mother's journals as they worked to understand what had happened and tried to understand business information she had included in them.

They had been completely surprised to learn about the gold nuggets Mother had found before they were born. Laura and Talon had continued to find nuggets for years afterward. Laura made annual trips to Denver to take the nuggets to her banker.

She also visited her lawyer for updates on the business dealings he took care of in her absence. Her business dealings? That had been a shocker. They had always thought of their mother as a horse rancher. However, they realized anytime the ranch needed something major, Laura had always been able to provide it.

In their ignorance, they thought the ranch supported itself. Their Appaloosa horses were in big demand, and they thought that was where all the extra money came from. Now they knew differently but not enough. They needed to know all in order to take care of the family business.

Black Hawk and Raven were not here, and they had no idea when they would be available. It was up to them to take care of it. They had already let a year pass since their mother had died. They knew they had lost valuable time.

As they ate a late supper at the ranch house, they made plans to go to Denver tomorrow to see the lawyer, Samuel Miller, and visit the bank. For the first time since their mother died, they felt they had a purpose. Both had felt adrift in a storm whirling above their heads. They discussed what to do about their siblings, since they were not here.

"Black Hawk could walk in at any time, but at this time of year, he would be hunting with the tribe and too difficult to find. We have no way of contacting him. We will let Raven know when we know more."

They were in agreement with the plan.

Shortly after noon the next day, Will and Eli walked into Mr. Miller's office in Denver. He was glad to meet them when they told him who they were. He ushered them into his office, closing the door behind him.

"How may I help you?" he asked, afraid of the answer since Laura was not with them.

"Our mother has passed away. She left instructions for us to contact you for more information regarding her estate and business dealings," Will managed to get out.

Eli nodded.

"I am sorry for your loss. Your mother was a wonderful woman. She was a smart businesswoman and a longtime friend. Are you aware of her holdings?" Mr. Miller asked as he looked at both of Laura's handsome sons.

"Her holdings?" they said in stunned unison.

"I see you are surprised. You will truly be amazed when I read her will and you learn the extent of all you and your siblings now own," he said with a sincere smile on his face.

Rising from his chair, he went over to the large vault he had installed when he had built his office building. Denver had continued to grow by leaps and bounds after the railroad came to town. Because of his business associations with Laura, he had grown quite wealthy. She had always trusted him, and he had dealt with her honestly and fairly. She had trusted him with her many secrets, too.

"Where are the other two children? Black Hawk and Raven?" he asked as he removed her file from his safe and settled it on his desk.

Her sons stared at the thickness of it.

"We are not sure where Black Hawk is. He is with his tribe hunting somewhere. Raven is still back East. We have not heard from her since Mother passed a year ago," replied Will.

Surprised at the length of time since Laura's death, Mr. Miller regained his composure and said, "We really should have everyone present, but under the circumstances, I understand." He opened the file, lifted out Laura's last will and testament, and read it to her sons.

They sat in dazed silence for a while before Mr. Miller asked, "Do you have any questions?"

Eli asked in disbelief, "Our mother purchased land around Denver, and now we own lots and buildings here in town?"

"That's right. She used the gold to increase her holdings here and allowed me to buy land for her as I saw fit. She trusted me to make investments for her, and I hope you will be happy with the investments I have made on her behalf. She had me buy properties in her name as well as those of each of her children.

"Therefore, as she acquired a new property in her name, one of your names went on the deed also. That way, if something happened to her, her children would own the property outright. Here is a list of the properties you own and a list of properties Eli owns." As he handed them each a sheet of paper, he went over what each owned.

Strong feelings of love rose in both men as they realized what their mother had done for them. It was difficult for them to grasp they were now wealthy. Will managed to ask, "Do Black Hawk and Raven have a list of their properties as well?"

"Oh yes, here are their lists," Mr. Miller answered as he handed them the other two lists of properties. "And besides the properties, each of you has a bank account where rents from your properties are deposited."

The lawyer continued. "Many people have inquired if we would sell any of the properties. I have insisted they are not for sale, but now that you and your siblings know about them, you may want me to sell them for you. That is something I would encourage you not to do right now. These properties are good moneymakers. Denver continues to grow with paved streets and gaslights springing up everywhere. The railroad has brought industry to us. If in the future you want to sell, we can discuss the pros and cons about doing that."

He watched the expressions play over their faces as he asked, "Are you fully aware of the size of the horse ranch?"

"What do you mean?" Will asked as he looked up.

"Your mother had continued to increase her land holdings of the ranch, and now it totals more than four thousand acres. She had me buying properties that touched your ranch until it grew quite large. She did insist the four of you own it together. In her will, you are not to sell it to a stranger, but if one or more wants out of the ranching business, it must be sold to the remaining sibling or siblings who want to stay on the ranch. She wanted it to stay in the family if possible. If everyone wants out, she has made provisions for a national park.

"However, she was concerned about Black Hawk and his people needing land to live on. She knew the world as we know it was changing, and she tried to foresee and adjust to the changes," he said as he explained her reasons for doing what she did.

Her sons nodded, still in shock from what they had learned.

Mr. Miller had also advised them their mother had set up a trust for Raven many years before, when she was a minor, and he was the trustee of it if anything should happen to Laura. He would continue to see she had funds to be able to remain in Washington with her aunt, if she chose.

Later as the brothers left the bank after visiting with the banker, they decided to get a room at the Ralston Hotel. They walked into the lobby in awe because they owned it and the land it sat on. They grinned at each other when they signed the register for two rooms. After agreeing to meet in the dining room for dinner, they went to their rooms to clean up.

The brothers were silent as they finished their meals, each digesting not only the food they had consumed, but also the day's events.

"Well, little brother, it seems you are a wealthy man. What are you going to do with all your wealth?" Will asked in jest.

Eli was slow in answering him, but when he did, it astonished both of them. "Well, I have been thinking I would like to search out my real father. I need to know more about him."

Will sucked in his breath as he looked at his brother, saying, "We are more alike than we realize because that is exactly what I was thinking about doing."

"Well, then we had better decide on how we are going to do this. Of course, you do realize we may find one or both dead by now. Then what would that do to us?"

"We have to know it may not turn out the way we want it to, but at least we will have tried. We need to know what happened to them after they left our mother. Remember, they do not even know we exist, so if they are alive, we could be a big shock to them and the families they have now," stated Will as he finished his pie and coffee.

"We need to make plans about contacting Black Hawk and Raven and about who will see to the ranch in our absence," replied Eli as he began mentally going over all the details to be taken care of before they could leave.

After they returned to the ranch the next day, they called a meeting with Matt Wilson, the ranch foreman; Sadie, her husband, John; and her sister, Marty, so they could explain what had been going on and what they were planning on doing.

Matt Wilson was the first to speak after they had told the group the news. In his soft-spoken voice, he said, "Now don't you two worry about the ranch while you are gone. You can rest assured I will take care of everything here just as I always have. When I returned after taking my mother back to Georgia, your mother promised me a job. I promised your mother when I was just a young'un she could always count on me. And you can, too."

Sadie had gotten her voice back by that time, and she replied, "Matt is right. This is something you boys need to do, and we will be right here to see to everything. You have to go find out about your fathers. Me, John, Marty, Matt, and his family will keep on with the ranching until you get back. Except what will we do if Black Hawk and Raven show up? You know Raven and me never got along very well. She didn't like me making her mind me; I switched her behind, just like I did with you two."

Loud hoots and laughter sounded in the room as they remembered the showdowns between Raven and the housekeeper.

"We'll leave letters for both, directing them to Mother's cabin. They need to go through the same process we have because if I know them, they have not grieved for Mother any better than we have. Will you see they do it if they come back before we do?" Will asked as he looked at each one.

They nodded in agreement.

Later, Will and Eli wrote the letters they would leave for their siblings in the event they returned to the ranch before them. After much heated debate over what to put in the letters, they finally agreed on what to tell their brother and sister. They left both on the large dining table and made Sadie promise she would not steam them open after they left.

Sadie promised with her fingers crossed behind her back.

Within four days, they were packed and headed for Denver with Matt riding along to bring back the horses. They had decided they could travel faster by train to San Antonio, Texas, and buy horses there. The Appaloosas were expensive horseflesh, and they did not want to fight to keep them. The only information they had was in the letters the men had left their mother.

Will's father, Jim McKenna, had said he was going to San Antonio, but that had been back in 1867. It was now 1889, and he could be anywhere or dead.

Eli's father, Rowdy Adams, had only indicated he would be heading where Jim was going. What if he did not go there at all? They would have to go and see what they could find.

After buying their tickets at the train station, they shook hands with Matt, thanking him for seeing them off. Before boarding the train, the brothers sent a telegram to Raven, letting her know what they were planning.

Finding seats in the passenger car, securing their satchels under their seats, they settled down for a long ride through Colorado, New Mexico, and halfway across Texas. Having never been farther than Denver, they were nervous but thankful they had each other for comfort.

7

The Twins

A grueling week later, Will and Eli stepped off the train in San Antonio, Texas. They were expecting a frontier town, but a bustling city almost as large as Denver and still growing greeted them. Every place the railroad went, it brought prosperity.

Expecting to make a few inquiries at the local saloon to locate someone who knew of Jim McKenna or Rowdy Adams now seemed out of the question. They were trying to decide what to do next when someone called to them from the busy street.

A man with a carriage for hire agreed to drive them to a good hotel in the main part of town for six bits.

"What hotel would you recommend?" asked Will as he and Eli climbed into the open carriage.

"If you can afford it, I would say the Menger. It is downtown and redone just last year. It is very fancy with good eating places nearby and near the famous Alamo," he said as he spit a stream of tobacco juice in the road while he waited for them to settle.

"What's the Alamo?" Will asked as he got out of the carriage in front of the impressive hotel, looking up and down the cobblestone street.

The driver looked at Will as if he had crawled out from under a rock as he said, "One of the most important battles took place right here between Santa Anna and volunteers, which freed us from Mexican rule, and you ask that stupid question? If you are going to stay long, better brush up on your Texas history, mister."

"Thanks for the information. I will. Is there a livery stable nearby?"

"Yep, right down from the Menger on the right. Can't miss it. It's near the end of the street."

"Much obliged to you," Will said. He paid the man and waved goodbye as the man whistled to the horses. The deafening noises from wagon wheels and horses' hooves on the busy cobbled streets hurried them inside.

Carrying their satchels into the lavish hotel lobby, they looked around as they approached the front desk, immediately feeling the coolness inside compared to the hot Texas heat. Exotic Persian carpets covered the floor, colorful Paris oil paintings hung on the walls, and palm trees grew in large pots throughout the lobby.

After asking for adjoining rooms with baths, they were delighted when they were accommodated with a suite. They did not know what that was, but the desk clerk was quick to explain to them they would have a living room, two separate bedrooms, and a large bathing room. Room service was also available if they preferred to dine in the suite.

Sending amazed glances at each other, they found it difficult to believe they were here in San Antonio and they could afford to stay in a luxury hotel. But they planned to enjoy every minute of it while they could.

They knew when they returned to their simple way of life, they would go back to running their horse ranch. Of course, a lot depended on what they found out here, too.

They looked and felt like country bumpkins as they followed the bellhop to their rooms. Surprised at the size of their suite and the opulent furnishings, they could not hide their excitement. But the most shocking thing for them was the marble bathing room. Hot and cold water came out of faucets connected above the tub.

"I could get used to this luxury, Will. No more hauling buckets of water to take a bath. How about you?"

"Amazing."

The adjoining rooms were appointed with more of the expensive carpets, paintings, and flocked wallpaper, just like the lobby. For the first time in their lives, they were experiencing luxury.

Several hours later, after they had soaked the long train trip out of their bones, the brothers went downstairs to eat in the dining room. While they waited for their steaks to be prepared, they overheard two men discussing a cattle rustling that had occurred in the area.

After the men left, Will asked the waitress who they were. She replied, "The tall one is Sheriff Clancy and the shorter man is Captain Frank Jones of the Texas Rangers."

"What are Texas Rangers?"

"You have never heard of the Texas Rangers? They are the fiercest lawmen ever! If there is trouble, all you need is one Texas Ranger to take care of it," she said proudly.

"We are looking for two men. Perhaps you might know them—Jim McKenna and Rowdy Adams."

The waitress looked surprised for a moment, then said in a whisper, "You should talk to Captain Jones." She filled their coffee cups and quickly moved away.

Will and Eli glanced at each other in bewilderment. Perhaps the waitress had reacted that way because the men they sought were outlaws and she didn't want to get involved.

After they finished their meal, they left the hotel to check out the livery stable. A young stable boy showed them the horses for sale, but he did not know the prices.

"I'll run and get the owner, and he can tell you," he yelled over his shoulder as he hurried into the barn.

"I'm disappointed in what I see. There is not one among them that I would want to own," Will remarked to Eli as the owner approached.

"Sorry to hear that. This is all I got now until someone brings me more to sell or trade." The horse trader waved his hand over the lot of them.

"What brings you to San Antonio?" he inquired. He never missed an opportunity to find out information before anyone else.

Eli was quick to ask, "What makes you think we are not from around here?"

Sweat popped out of the horse seller's forehead when he realized he might have overstepped himself. He quickly replied, "Well, you do not have the Texas drawl, and I just thought you might be from someplace else. I don't want no trouble, mister. Just trying to be friendly."

"No offense taken. Do you know when you will get more horses or where we can find some of better quality?" Will asked him, not answering any of the man's questions.

"I will be happy to rent you horses and give you directions to a ranch a ways out of town that might have what you are looking for," he replied as they walked back into the shade of the barn, since the day had grown hotter.

"How far is the horse ranch from here?" questioned Eli.

"It's about an hour's ride out of town. Not sure if they have any for sale, but they might," answered the man as he wiped his sweating forehead with his dirty handkerchief.

"We'll be back in the morning. Please have the horses saddled, and we will get directions from you than," Will said as he gave the man half the money for the rentals.

As the brothers walked down Main Street, looking for the Ranger office, Will realized they were being followed. He stopped suddenly to look in the mercantile store window. Eli almost collided with him.

"Why did you stop like that? What's so interesting in the millinery window?" he asked, irritated at his brother.

Will pointed at something in the window as he said in a low whisper, "Don't look around. Someone has been trailing us since we left the hotel and now the livery. When we get to the corner, duck into the alley. We will see who is following us and why," he said as he straightened and continued on down the boardwalk.

As they neared the corner, they walked faster and turned into the alley, hiding behind some boxes piled there. Fast footsteps hurried down the alley to see where they had gone.

When the man walked past their hiding place, the brothers stepped out, cocking their guns.

Hearing the guns click, the man raised his hands and said, "Don't shoot!"

"Who are you, and why are you following us? Did you think you could rob us?" asked Will in an angry voice.

"Just following orders," replied the man as he turned slowly around with his hands still in the air. A strange-looking badge was pinned to his shirt.

"Whose orders? Who do you work for?" Eli asked, then heard a gun cock behind them.

"Drop your guns slowly," came the order from behind them.

As they released the hammers on their weapons, they let them slowly slide to the ground.

"Who are you, and why are you following us?" Will asked the man behind them.

"Turn around slowly, both of you," was the order from behind.

Turning with their hands in the air, they saw the man who had the drop on them and recognized him.

"Captain Jones, we were just coming to your office when we discovered we were being followed and ducked in here."

"What's your name? And how do you know me?" Captain Jones asked suspiciously.

"We, uh...are brothers from Colorado. I am Will Ralston, and this is my brother, Eli. We don't talk very well with our hands in the air, sir," continued Will. "Could we go to your office for a private conversation?"

Captain Jones studied both men as a strange look came across his face. "All right, lower your hands, and we will talk in my office." He signaled the other man to pick up their guns and follow them.

Soon they were in the captain's office and seated on wooden chairs in front of his desk. "What are you men looking to find here? I know you have been asking questions."

"We saw you in the hotel when we first arrived and asked who you were. How did that get back to you so quickly?" asked Eli.

"I saw you both in the hotel as well and knew you did not come from around here. I have been a lawman for a long time, and I am observant of strangers. Even though San Antonio is growing rapidly, we still try to watch out for suspicious gunslingers."

Will laughed at the notion they might be gunslingers. "We are horse ranchers from Colorado, looking to open up a market for our horses here. We are not gunslingers, but we can protect ourselves if we have to."

Eli looked surprised at Will's statement but added, "Since you are a lawman, we are sure you need good, dependable horseflesh. We have some of the best."

Captain Jones continued to observe the men. He was good at knowing what kind of man he was dealing with. Both seemed to be what they were saying, and yet he sensed they had not told him all the truth. They were holding back something, and he was determined to find out what. And they looked so familiar to him.

"Well, you are right about my rangers needing good mounts. They must be rugged and very dependable. We'll talk more about the horses you want to sell. Sorry we thought you were outlaws," he said. He laughed as he returned their guns.

"You are free to go."

The men rose and shook Captain Jones's hand before they quickly exited the Ranger office. Will shook his head at Eli so he would not say anything until they were sure they could talk in private.

They locked the door to their suite, and then spoke in lower tones to each other.

"What was that all about? Why did you use Mother's maiden name? Why did you tell him we are horses traders? And why didn't you ask him if he knew our fathers?" Eli asked.

"I don't think he fully believed us. He probably heard from the waitress who we are looking for. I don't know why, but it seemed he might be trying to protect them. We will have to be careful from now on until we can get more information. Let's rest now, and tomorrow we will ride out to see if we can find some decent horses."

"Good idea. I'm beat and will say good night."

8

Captain Jones

Captain Jones watched the men cross the street as they headed toward their hotel. He left San Antonio soon after, riding south toward a friend's ranch. He wanted to talk to his good friend about something that was bothering him.

An hour later, he rode through the ranch gate with the overhead brand of "Forever Ranch" in iron letters. He always wondered why his friend named his ranch that. But minding his own business, he never asked.

The dogs barked a warning to the ranch that someone was coming. He waited until the dogs were called off before climbing down from his horse. Ranch guard dogs were vicious, and he didn't want to be bitten. The housekeeper and a ranch hand had hurried to quiet the dogs when they saw who it was and signaled he could come up on the porch.

"Hello, Mary Lee. How is he today?" he asked her softly.

Mary Lee's eyes filled with tears. "Captain Jones, he just lies there in a deep depression. I don't know how to reach him. I am so glad you came."

"How is his leg?"

"Doc Farley has done all he can do. We are still trying to get the infection under control, but I can't get him to get up. He runs a high fever at times. He has lost the will to live. He will barely eat or even let me help him. If something doesn't happen soon, he may lose his leg." Her voice broke, and she wiped a tear with the corner of her apron.

Captain Jones patted her hand and headed down the hall to his friend's bedroom. Opening the door to the darkened room, he was surprised and heartbroken at the major changes in his friend.

Lying in the middle of a giant four-poster bed was a large man. His eyes were closed and sunk deeply into the sockets. A deathly pallor replaced his usual robust color.

When Jim heard the door open, he roared, "Go away and leave me alone. I don't want anything, and I don't need anything."

"That's not a nice greeting for an old friend, now is it, you son of a bitch?"

Instantly recognizing Frank's voice, he said vehemently, "Go away. I don't need your sympathy, either."

"Well, good, because you were not going to get it. I want you out of that bed now. You are a Texas Ranger, and I need you to get back to work. I'm tired of your lollygagging and not working. I need help, Jim," Frank roared back.

"Get out of my house, you bastard."

"Only way I am leaving is if you put me out," Frank said as he got comfortable in the rocking chair before the cold fireplace.

Jim heard the squeak of the old wooden rocker as Frank rocked. He waited for a while, hoping Frank would give up and leave, but he knew he was too damn stubborn to do that.

In desperation he said, "Why are you here bothering me? You know I will never be able to be a Ranger again. So why waste my time and yours?"

The rocker stopped as Frank rose. The floorboards creaked as leather boots walked toward his bed. Jim heard the faint jingle of silver rowels on his friend's spurs with each step before Frank stopped near his bed.

He squeezed his eyes shut, not wanting to see the pity in his friend's eyes. He waited, but Frank did not move or say anything to him.

"What are you waiting for?" he yelled out. But only silence followed.

Jim jumped at the closeness of Frank's voice when he whispered near his ear, "I am waiting for you to open your eyes and look at me. You won't see pity or sympathy from me but respect for a strong Texas Ranger who is bouncing on a rough road right now."

Jim slowly opened his eyes and looked at his best friend for the first time since he had been shot—and Rachael had been killed—and his world had ceased to exist anymore.

"Jim, we need to talk about the shooting and some other things that have happened lately. Will you get out of bed so we can?"

"I can't, Frank. Don't you understand I have nothing to live for now? Rachael is gone."

"Jim, I know you hurt, but you and Rachael have children who need you. They are grieving as well and are afraid they will lose you, too. Rachael would not want you to leave the children all alone, now would she?" Frank said softly.

Jim laid his head back on the pillow, squeezing his eyes shut again, not wanting to remember the horrible scene.

Frank waited until Jim said, "You are right, but I am so broken with her loss. I just don't know how to go on."

"Perhaps it would help to talk about it, and you could give me details about what exactly happened. What you remember. We are still trying to track them but haven't had much success. Not sure who or what they were after. Do you have any ideas?"

Jim rose on his elbows and looked Frank in the eyes as he said, "You will not go away until I get up, will you?"

Frank laughed. "No, my friend, I will not. You mean too much to me to leave you like this. Now get your ass up."

Frank pulled the bed covers back and helped Jim slide his legs to the edge of the bed.

"Can you put any weight on your leg?"

"I don't know. Will you help me so I don't fall?"

Frank grabbed his left arm so Jim would have support for his injured left leg. Guided toward the rocking chair, Jim was able to limp along and ease into the chair. Exhausted from the few steps from the bed to the chair, he looked sadly at his friend. "See, I can't even support myself."

"That was great. You are up and moving. Of course, it will be slow at first, but you will make it. Now, tell me in your own words what happened that day."

Jim's eyes glazed over at the happy memories, and then the terrible scenes played out before his eyes. He was silent for a while before he began.

"Rachael and the children had left the ranch early in the buckboard and were meeting me on the road to Rowdy's ranch for an Easter Sunday lunch and visit. We hadn't seen them for a while. With the weather holding up so nicely, it was a wonderful spring day. As we drove up to his ranch house, Rowdy and his family came out of the house to greet us.

"We were yelling greetings to each other as my family began to climb down from the wagon. Before I could dismount from my horse, shots rang out, and a group of riders descended on us. My horse reeled as I was hit in the left leg and knocked off, dazed and blinded by all the dust stirred up by the outlaws' horses." Jim drew several deep breaths before continuing.

"More gunshots, screaming, and blood everywhere. I couldn't get to my feet, so I dragged myself over to where Rachael lay on the ground. One of the sons of bitches shot her between the eyes, Frank. She was dead before she hit the ground. I held her in my arms, even though the shots and screams continued around me. What kind of man am I to not have tried to protect my children and Rowdy's family as well? I just sat there, holding Rachael in my arms and crying like a baby."

Silence followed his question.

Finally, Frank said, "Everyone reacts differently to bad situations. Do you think Rowdy or any of us would accuse you of not doing enough? No, because we might have done the same thing. You lost your love in an act of vengefulness. I can't think of anything more devastating."

"How is Rowdy? I have refused to see anyone since the attack. I have been so into my sorrows, I never asked if he and his family were all right," Jim asked with deep sorrow in his voice.

Frank raised his head to look at Jim. "Then you don't know? The outlaws took his oldest daughter, Emily Rose, when they left. A bullet grazed Rowdy's head, and he was knocked out and couldn't follow. He was unconscious for several days before he finally came around. He suffers from terrible headaches that send him to his bed. And of course, his heart is heavy for his daughter and for your loss. He doesn't know if they were after him or both of you. There wasn't anything to indicate who they were or whom they were working for. It could have been a random attack. Do you remember anything you might have seen or heard that could be of help to us?"

Jim closed his eyes, thinking of the tragic events that day. Suddenly, he opened his eyes and looked directly at Frank. "I heard one of the men say, 'Blackjack will be happy about us taking out both of them.' So they must have been after Rowdy and me."

"Do you think he was speaking of Blackjack Ketchum?"

"We did have some trouble with him sometime back. One of us shot him, but he got away. Later we heard he was somewhere in New Mexico. Do you think he planned this?"

"Don't know if he planned it or somebody was wanting to get in good with Blackjack and did it on his own. But that will give us something to go on. Do you know anyone named Ralston?"

"No, why?"

"Two men have shown up, asking questions about you and Rowdy. They said they were horse traders, but I have a hunch about them."

Jim shifted in his chair and gasped when he moved his leg the wrong way.

"Let me help you to the dining table. It's about time for supper, and I don't want to eat without you. I know your children will be glad to see you are up. Come on."

Before Jim could argue, Frank had him on his feet and limping to the dining table.

During dinner, Frank carried the conversation with humorous stories about Jim and himself working as Rangers together. The children were pleased to have their father at the supper table.

Mary Lee got Jim some soup, but he refused to eat it. His fever continued to linger, and before the others had finished dinner, Jim asked, "Frank, will you please take me back to my bed?"

When Frank prepared to leave after he helped Jim back to bed, Susan, Jim's oldest, was waiting to hand him his hat.

"We are so glad you came to supper and Father joined us for a while. It has been lonely without him and Mother," Susan said as she brushed a tear from her eye.

His youngest son, James, asked, "Uncle Frank, will you come back soon?"

"I'll be back as soon as I can, James. Mary Lee is a wonderful cook, and I don't want to miss out on another slice of her apple pie."

After Frank said his goodbyes, he headed back to town. As he rode, he contemplated what Jim had told him. He would start checking up on Blackjack Ketchum tomorrow.

9

The Twins

When Will and Eli left the hotel the next morning, they went to the livery stable to get their horses and the directions to the ranch. They were directed to travel east along the San Antonio River to the end of the road. When they got to the ranch, they were to ask for Shorty, the foreman.

At the ranch entrance, they stared at the huge rock entrance. It was built of sandstone with a large metal gate. But what had stopped them in their tracks was the name of the ranch. A mountain scene had been worked into the metal gate, and ornate green letters proclaimed "Rocky Mountain Ranch."

They looked at each other strangely.

"Are you as surprised as I am to find something like this here? Makes me wonder who owns the ranch," Will said.

Eli replied, "Very surprised. I wish we had asked more questions of the livery man. What should we do?"

Will thought for a moment, then said, "We are horse buyers who have come out looking for some good horses. That's all we need to say. We

41

will wait to see what we find here. It may be nothing, but then it may be another clue on our treasure hunt."

Eli laughed. "Our treasure hunt. Yes, that is what this is, isn't it?" He clicked to his horse as he opened the big gate, allowing them to move through, and then closed it behind them.

When they approached the barn and corral, ranch hands were sitting atop the corral, whooping at a cowboy on a bucking horse in the middle of the arena. The rider's hat was pulled down almost over his ears, and he gripped a rein in each hand, spurring the horse each time it leaped in the air.

Will and Eli were mesmerized because the cowboy seemed to be one with the horse, glued to the saddle and not coming off. Finally winded, the horse ceased to pitch. Turning the horse this way and that way, the rider forced it to obey the commands of the reins with guidance from his strong legs and spurs.

A loud cheer went up as the cowboy circled the corral and pulled the horse up to the fence. He got down near where Will and Eli were standing and handed the reins to one of the other cowboys as he came through the gate near them.

"Good ride, cowboy," Will said just as the cowboy pulled her sweat-stained hat from her head and long red hair flowed over her shoulders.

"Thanks, mister. I raised that stud from a colt and have looked forward to the time I could break him. He will be a great ride when I'm through with him," she said as her green eyes looked up into his dark sapphire ones.

Will's heart stopped. His breathing stopped. He was dying as her spirit overwhelmed his senses. All he was able to do was stare down at her as he swam in her beautiful emerald eyes. Flaming red hair and cool green eyes...He was lost.

"I'm Hannah Adams. Do I know you? You look so familiar. What is your name?"

Eli had been staring down at her as well and wasn't at all surprised Will had lost his voice. Hannah Adams was beautiful, even dressed as a sweaty and dusty cowboy, and was possibly his sister.

"My name is Eli Ralston, and this door knocker is my brother Will. We came out here looking to buy a couple of horses. We were told you might have some for sale. Are we at the right place?"

Will quickly recovered. "What do you want for the one you were riding?"

"Oh, he's not for sale. He's mine."

"Are you the owner of the ranch?"

"No, my father is, but he allows me to have the say of the horses. We raise top stock and don't want them sold to just anyone who would use them as plow horses."

Both men laughed. "Our mother always said that about our horses, too. We have a horse ranch in Colorado and raise a special breed called Appaloosas. Have you heard of them?"

"No, but that is interesting. Would you like to come to the house and talk to Father? He...uh...hasn't been getting out much lately."

"Yes, ma'am. Lead the way."

As Hannah led the way to the house, Will couldn't keep his eyes off her cute little butt. She may have been dressed in men's clothes, but she sent his heart to pounding anytime he looked at her—like now, as he watched the cadence of her hips move in time with the jiggle in her jeans and the jingle of her spurs.

Eli gave him a sharp elbow to his ribs and a dirty look when he saw what he was staring at.

"Mother! Father! We have company," Hannah yelled as she led the way into the spacious living room. Immediately the room came to life with people large and small gathering around the newcomers.

"Father, this is Will and Eli Ralston from Colorado. They are here to buy horses from us."

Rowdy had started to extend his hand in greeting but froze as he looked fully at Will, recognizing his friend Jim as a young man. Turning his eyes upon Eli created a swirling sensation beginning in his stomach, surging and burning upward to surround his heart, gripping it as if it had fingers of fire. There standing before him was a younger version of himself.

How was this possible? Who were these men?

"Father, are you all right? You look pale. Is your head hurting you again?"

Finally extending his hand to shake Will's and Eli's, he nodded a greeting as he tried to regain his voice. His mind reeled with so many questions.

Eli was experiencing some of the same emotions as Rowdy. He felt he was looking in a mirror and seeing himself in twenty years.

As the silence in the room grew louder, Rowdy's wife, Ruth, stepped forward and introduced their other children. "You have already met Hannah; this is David, Andrew, Daniel, and Katie. And I'm Mrs. Adams. Won't you please sit down?"

Sending Hannah and the other children to the kitchen for refreshments, she said, "Rowdy, I believe you and Jim have some explaining to do."

When he did not respond, she said, "Where are you young men from?"

Will regained his voice before Eli. "Ma'am, we are from Denver, Colorado. We have the Spotted Horse Ranch there. But we came to Texas by train on business and needed horses once we got here. The livery man sent us to your ranch to see if you had any for sale."

There was another long pause, and only the sounds of children's voices and clinking dishes could be heard from the kitchen.

Clearing his throat, Rowdy asked, "Who is your mother?"

After a much longer pause, Will answered, "Laura Ralston Brown. Do you know her?"

Rowdy leaped to his feet and hurried from the room. Ruth stared at the young men who had invaded her living room and her life.

"How is your mother? Is she with you?" she asked softly, fearing the answers.

"Mrs. Adams, we did not come here to cause any trouble but to find answers. Our mother passed last year, and we recently found out we have separate fathers. Do you think you could get Mr. Adams to talk with us? Then we will go."

"Rowdy loved your mother very much. It took him a long time to get over her, but he never stopped loving her. It has been said you never get over your first true love. And by his reactions, you can see that is true. I will talk to him. Would you stay for dinner before you ride back into town?"

"Thank you, but we will leave now. If he wants to talk with us, we are at the Menger. It was nice meeting you, Mrs. Adams."

The men left, duly shaken by the meeting. It was apparent Rowdy Adams was Eli's father, but what about Will's? They did not get to talk with Rowdy about Jim McKenna and what had happened to him. Back at the hotel, the brothers went to their bedrooms, agreeing to meet later for dinner.

Hours later a knock sounded on their door. Will opened it, surprised but pleased to see Rowdy Adams standing there.

"May I come in?"

Opening the door wider, Will stepped aside to allow him in. Calling Eli from his bedroom, he said, "Eli, we have a visitor."

Hurrying into the room, Eli stopped short when he saw Rowdy. "We did not come to cause any problems for you and your family. We only want answers, sir."

"May I sit down? Not sure my legs will continue to hold me up. I am shaken to the core by your appearance. I did not know about you. Please believe me."

Will motioned for him to take the chair so Eli could sit in the other chair nearest him while Will sat on the couch, not wanting to miss a single word.

"Ruth told me what you said, and she insisted I come and talk with you. I loved your mother very much. I wanted to marry her and help her save the ranch. But she was headstrong and refused to marry Jim or me. She would not let either of us stay with her. I left her a letter with information about my family and where I would be if she ever needed me. I had hoped she would write me to come back if she was expecting my child, but it never happened. And now I see myself in a young man who is her son. My son," he whispered as the emotion shook him.

Eli spoke for the first time. "Yes, she was headstrong and determined to make it on her own terms. Sometime after you left, a storm knocked over a tree, dislodging a mother lode of gold nuggets. She gathered them, took them to Denver, and became very rich. We knew nothing about it until she had passed." His voice broke before he continued. "And we read her journals. We always lived modestly on the ranch. But the journals explained so much to us about our mother and about ourselves. We are twins but so different. We found out she had two men—her angel men, she called them—whom she loved very much. Too much to choose one."

Rowdy put his face in his hands as he listened and grieved for the woman he had loved.

"After Mother died, we found her journals of her life and her loves. We also found a letter addressed to you and another to Jim McKenna. Do you know where Jim is? Is he still alive?"

Rowdy's head came up with a big smile on his face for the first time today. "Yes, to all your questions. But I have some of my own before I answer those. Tell me about your mother's life after we left. Did she ever marry? Are there other children? I need to know. I want to know she was happy."

"Perhaps if you read her letter, it might help with some of your questions. We do not know what she has written to you," Will told him as he handed it to him.

"Yes, let me read it. Thank you," he replied as he took the letter with shaking hands and lovingly opened it. It read:

> 1888
> My Dearest Rowdy,
>
> So much time has passed since I last kissed your handsome face on the saddest day of my life when I made you and Jim leave. It was impossible for me to choose between you because each of you was special and dear to me. I loved you so much. But I loved Jim just as much.
>
> I truly believed I was barren. Abner had convinced me. Imagine my excitement when I discovered I was with child by one of you. My first impulse was to write to both

of you, but I did not know whose child I carried. So I decided to wait until the baby was born, hoping I would be able to tell.

I was completely surprised when I gave birth to twin boys, each one looking like his father. But by that time, I had met Eagle Talon, whom I came to know was my soul mate. He loved the boys before they were born and was a caring father to them.

He has since died, taking my heart and soul with him. I am writing to say I'm sorry I hurt you. I understand how a love lost can feel. I pray in the future you will know and meet your son, Samuel Eli Adams Brown.

I have prayed always for your happiness,
My Angel Man,
Laura

Rowdy was visibly shaken after reading Laura's letter. But after a time, he gathered his thoughts and wits about him and said, "Laura was a good and godly woman. I never want anyone to think badly of her. And I don't want you to, either."

"Yes, sir, we agree with you."

They talked for hours before realizing it had grown late and they were hungry. Taking their visit downstairs to the dining area, they continued long into the night.

Since it was late when they finished talking, Rowdy got a room for the night. Before leaving them, he said, "I will take you out in the morning to meet Jim. He needs a surprise like this to help him want to live again. Since Easter morning when my Emily Rose was taken, Rachael McKenna was killed, and we were both shot, our lives have not been the same. You may have saved his life as well as mine."

10

Will

After an early breakfast, they rode with Rowdy to Jim's ranch. Will was apprehensive about meeting Jim. Uncertainty and doubt swirled in his mind as they continued the ride to the ranch.

How will he take meeting me? Am I good enough? These questions swirled in his mind, and he could not answer.

As they entered the gate to Jim's ranch, the name of the ranch jolted Will. He remembered the word *forever* had been carved with a heart around it on his mother's bench on the Widow's Peak. Could Jim have carved the word and named his ranch so as not to forget his Laura? More questions with no answers filled his brain as he rode under the arch and toward his future.

The ranch dogs sounded the alarm but grew unusually silent as Will, Eli, and Rowdy rode up to the front of the house. Rowdy looked down at the dogs and then around at the men with a questioning look.

Will smiled at him with a knowing look.

Rowdy knew Will had quieted the dogs. He remembered Laura's special powers with animals. As they stepped down from their horses, Mary

Lee called a greeting from the front porch to Rowdy to come on in but looked strangely at the vicious dogs that were jumping up and licking Will.

Hugging the housekeeper, Rowdy said, "Boys, this is Mary Lee, the housekeeper and best cook around. Mary Lee, this is Will and Eli Ralston." After making introductions, he asked, "How is he doing? Any better?"

"Frank was out yesterday and got him to get up and come to the table for a little while last night. But he didn't eat anything. Today he feels so bad he is not cooperating with anyone again."

"Mary Lee, will you get them some coffee and show them into the living room? I will go get Jim up."

"It is nice to meet you boys," she said, giving each a strange glance. "Please have a seat in there, and I will get you some coffee, unless you would prefer water."

"No, ma'am, coffee would be fine," Eli answered for both, since he could tell Will was too nervous to say anything.

Rowdy went down the hallway and into a bedroom near the staircase. In a few minutes, loud, angry voices could be heard from the direction he had gone in, and sounds of breaking glass echoed in the stillness.

In a soft whisper, Will said, "I guess he is not taking finding out about me very well."

"You don't know if that is why he is angry and arguing with Rowdy. Be patient. He'll come out."

More yelling and loud cussing followed Eli's comment, then silence. Finally, a door opened, and there came the slow clopping of wood on wood and heavy breathing as the sounds moved closer to where the brothers waited.

"Damn, Jim, you stink. When have you had a bath?"

"None of your sorry-ass business. I wish everyone would leave me the hell alone and let me die in peace."

When Jim appeared in the doorway, he was dressed in his stained nightshirt. He leaned heavily on a crutch while Rowdy supported him on his left side. He was white faced from the strain, the pain, and the effort to walk.

"Who the hell is here, Rowdy? Why the hell are you making me get up and walk? I don't want to be here!" Jim shouted as his eyes fell on Will. Then he went limp as he looked at himself twenty years ago.

The brothers leaped to grab him before he fell. They maneuvered him over to the large leather chair Mary Lee had filled with down pillows and settled him in, propping his legs up on a large footrest that matched the dark leather chair.

Jim stared at Will. He felt as if he were looking in a mirror of himself. *What a horrible joke Rowdy was playing on him! And in his condition...He was on his deathbed, and Rowdy had dragged him out there.*

"Who the hell is this? Some kind of joke, Rowdy?" Jim lashed out angrily at his lifelong friend.

Nothing but silence filled the room. Rowdy was so disappointed in Jim's reaction. He couldn't bring himself to say anything. The brothers' faces were closed, and their emotions were hidden.

Will regained his composure and stood in front of Jim's chair as he extended his right hand in greeting, saying, "My name is James William McKenna Brown. But you may call me Will. Are you my father?"

Taking the direct approach seemed the best solution at the time. Jim, in shock from the turn of events, couldn't raise his hand to shake Will's. Time moved slowly, and the ticking of the large grandfather clock in the foyer could be heard as the four men stared at one another before Mary Lee swept into the room with cups of coffee and cookies. Will returned to sit on the couch when Jim did not shake his hand.

Sensing an undercurrent in the room, she chatted about the hot weather, the heavy rains, and the flooding of the river as she served the refreshments. She was trying everything to break the tension.

Rowdy accepted his coffee and sat down on the rock hearth near Jim. The brothers were given their cups as they sat side by side.

"I will have lunch in about an hour," Mary Lee stated as she left the tomblike room.

"So...you are Laura's son," Jim said as he found his tongue.

"We both are," replied Eli.

For the first time, Jim looked at the other young man in the room. Disbelief registered on his face as he recognized this man had the same coloring and features as his best friend, Rowdy. Rotating his head, he looked at Rowdy with a puzzled expression.

"We are twins," Will stated as he watched the memories show across Jim's face.

Turning to look at Rowdy again, Jim angrily yelled, "Why in hell didn't you warn me so I wouldn't make an ass of myself?"

Rowdy laughed good-naturedly as he said, "Well, I didn't have any warning, either. I went headfirst into it as well. They came to the ranch yesterday, looking to buy horses, and we discovered one another. Do you think Laura had anything to do with this? You know how mystical she was."

Jim shrugged as he turned to address Will. "Twins, you say. But you don't look alike. You look like Rowdy, and you look like me. Now I wonder how that happened."

"We read Mother's journals. We know how it happened. We have the same mother but two different fathers. We did not come here to cause you any problems with your families. We wanted to meet you both if you were still alive. Thank you for meeting us. We will not take up any more of your time," Will told him as he stood up to leave.

"You just wait a damn minute. You are not getting away so fast. I have questions, and I want answers, as I am sure you do, too. Please stay for lunch, and let's talk."

Will smiled for the first time that day as he held out Laura's letter to Jim, saying, "She wrote this to you before she died."

Staring at the letter before taking it, he looked down at the way Laura had written his name in her beautiful script. He looked at Rowdy, who nodded as he said, "I got one, too. It will do you good to read it. The boys and I will go out on the front porch so you can have your privacy."

Jim nodded as he stared at the letter again.

The men rose, took their coffee cups out to the porch, and sat down in the wooden rocking chairs, hoping to catch a cool breeze.

Sometime later, Mary Lee called them to the table. After helping Jim into the dining room, they propped up his bad leg on a chair.

"You still stink, Jim. If Mary Lee's cooking wasn't so good, I think I would leave. After we eat, we will be having a 'come to Jesus' meeting because like it or not, you are taking a bath," Rowdy told him.

Jim just grunted. Trying to change the subject, he introduced the brothers to his children. "Will and Eli, I want you to meet my children. The pretty one is Susan, then George, Charlie, Frank, and last but not least is James, who is five years old."

The brothers nodded at the children.

"I am concerned about Jim's leg wound. It is badly infected, and he keeps running a high fever," added Mary Lee as she served the men and children seated at the table.

Susan did not add to the conversation but glanced shyly at Eli when she thought he was not looking as she helped Mary Lee place large bowls filled with red beans, Mexican rice, gravy, and mashed potatoes; large platters of fried steak along with freshly made tortillas; and small bowls of hot sauce. The smells from the food were delicious.

Everyone waited for Mary Lee and Susan to be seated at the large table before grasping hands as Jim led them in a prayer, thanking God for the food and for His many blessings.

"Our grandmother, Running Fawn, is the Ute tribal medicine woman. She taught our father his healing skills and also our younger brother and us. If you will permit us to look at your wound, perhaps we might be able to help you," Will stated to Jim.

"Your father?" Jim asked. "Will you tell us about him? Was he good to your mother?"

Eli spoke first because he sensed Will could not. "He was Eagle Talon of the Southern Ute Nation. He was a very powerful and spiritual medicine man. He raised Will and me as if we were his own, and he loved our mother very much. We have another brother, Black Hawk, and a sister, who is Raven. We were raised in both worlds and allowed to choose our paths. Will and I were better horse ranchers than Indians. But Black Hawk has powerful medicine, as did his father. He still walks both paths, unable to choose."

"And your sister, Raven?"

"She was sent to Mother's sister, Auntie Jane, who lives in Washington, to be taught to be a lady because she has such a wild spirit. We know our aunt has had her hands full." The brothers laughed.

George spoke for the first time. "Like Hannah?"

"George, apologize to Rowdy," scolded Jim.

"But it's true. I have let her become one of the boys because she wants to please me," agreed Rowdy.

"But tell us why you laughed at your sister." Rowdy had looked at the merriment in their faces and wanted to be let in on their joke.

Will's laughter quieted. "It broke Mother's heart to send her away, but Father had been killed in a hunting accident, and no one could control her. She wanted to ride all day with her Indian cousins, and that was not the proper thing for a woman to do. She needed to be taught knowledge before she could truly choose her own path. She is still there."

Jim and Rowdy looked at each other, duly impressed with the love and sacrifices Laura had made for her children.

When the meal was over, Rowdy said, "We would love to hear more about your family, but Jim has got to have a bath. Mary Lee, heat up the water, and I'll get the tub and put it on the back porch." He rose to get things ready to bathe Jim.

Sometime later, after much cussing from Jim, the men had stripped him, bathed him, and redressed him in a clean nightshirt. When they got him out of the one he had lived in for weeks, Mary Lee grabbed it by her fingertips, holding her nose, and hurried out to burn the filthy nightshirt as well as the bed linens he would not allow her to change.

Jim was large, and it took all three of the men to bathe him and get him back to bed. His strength gave out long before they were done.

"Sir, will you allow us to look at your wound now?" Will asked as they placed him on his clean bed.

"I'm so tired. How about later?"

"Well, sir, if it is as bad as it smells, it needs immediate attention. I think gangrene has set up in it. You could lose your leg if it's not tended to immediately."

A desperate cry of agony came from Jim's lips. "Why am I so cursed? What did I do to deserve all this pain and heartache since Easter?"

"It is nothing we have done or not done that causes tragedy in our lives. We were not expecting Mother to die when she did, and it tore our world apart," commented Will.

"Well, go ahead and look at the leg. I'm a dead man anyway," he said in a whisper.

Jim turned on his right side to allow them to get a better look at his leg wound, located near his left hipbone. An ugly, gaping hole showed the exposed leg bone and oozed with stinking pus. Even after the bath, the infection was apparent.

"Eli and I can help you if you will agree to allow us to treat you with Indian medicines and ways."

With a loud sigh, Jim said, "At this point, I really don't care. The doc hasn't been very successful. Why not? If my leg comes off, I will not live like that."

"We understand, sir. We have ways of healing that white people do not know about. We will be back shortly to begin, but first we must gather what we need."

Both turned and left the room.

11

Jim

When the brothers returned, they were carrying several beaded leather pouches and a jar containing tiny white moving creatures. They had been gone long enough for Jim to fall asleep from his exertion.

Shaking him awake, Will said, "Mary Lee is preparing a tea for you to drink."

"I don't want no tea!" Jim growled.

As Mary Lee came into the room, Will told him, "This is one of Mother's herbal teas and will help bring down your fever. Please drink it."

Without further argument, he allowed them to help him sit up, and he drank it down as quickly as possible. Then, as Jim reclined on his right side, Will exposed the left leg so he and Eli could examine the wound better.

It was bad. The bullet had ripped through his leg, exiting on the other side. That was the good news. The bad news was gangrene had set up in the wounds, and brownish to red streaks were already streaming from his hip down his leg. The wound oozed smelly pus from both bullet holes.

Will shook tiny, white, wiggly creatures into the wound. As Jim felt them moving, he yelled, "What the hell are you putting on me? That looks like maggots! Oh shit! Get them out of there. They will eat my leg off!"

"Please lie still and trust me to know what I am doing. Last year one of our ranch hands cut his foot with an ax. He didn't say anything about the injury, and it got infected and gangrene set up before we knew what had happened. Black Hawk treated him the way I am treating you, and before the week was out, he was up and moving around. He did not lose his foot. The maggots will eat only the pus, not your healthy flesh. But if you truly want to die, I will remove them now."

There was a long pause before Jim said in a resigned voice, "Leave them."

"I will put a bandage on the wounds and change it tonight when I check on the progress. Sleep well, Jim. You need rest now."

Jim was asleep before anyone could leave the room.

Rowdy asked Eli, "Do you want to stay here tonight, or would you like to come home with me? You will have to sleep on the couch."

Taken by surprise from the invitation, Eli looked at Will. "If you are sure it will be fine with Mrs. Adams, and Eli wants to go, I think he should go. I will stay here to see to Jim's needs throughout the night and give Mary Lee some relief."

"Ruth and the children would like to become better acquainted with their new brother. You can do the same here with your new siblings, Will."

Rowdy and Eli left soon after thanking Mary Lee for a wonderful lunch. Susan watched Eli leave from the living room window. Something about him seemed to draw her to him. Was it his familiar looks or his strength of character that radiated he was a man of substance? Or was it his physical attributes that aroused her interest with wayward thoughts of kissing him on the lips? What would she do if he were interested in her in that way, too? The thoughts and images brought a big smile to her lips.

Jim slept soundly all night. Will did not bother him with checking the bandages because he knew the maggots were doing their job. He fell asleep on the settee in Jim's room and did not wake up until Mary Lee opened the bedroom door with cups of hot coffee early the next morning.

"How did he do in the night? He has not slept since the ambush," she whispered.

"He did not move much, and his breathing has stayed steady."

"I can hear you whispering about me. Do I smell coffee?"

Will approached Jim's bed and asked as Mary Lee handed him a cup, "How do you feel this morning?"

"I feel like my leg is full of creepy crawlies, but it may be because I know they are there. That's a terrible way to doctor someone."

"Hey, it works. Are you ready for me to look at it and see if I need to add fresh ones?"

"Fresh ones! Yeah, go ahead." Jim took several sips of his hot coffee before handing it back to Mary Lee and turning on his side so Will could remove the bandage and look at the wound.

Mary Lee gasped when she saw the maggots wiggling around in the pus but could tell it was improving and said so.

"Yes, it is looking better today. I will change them after lunch, and then you can have another nap. Mary Lee, after he has eaten breakfast, please give him more of the special tea. It will help with the fever."

"I will go fix breakfast, since you all are awake," Mary Lee said as she hurried out of the room.

Jim motioned for Will to come closer to him as he whispered, "I dreamed of your mother last night. At least I think it was a dream. She came to me and said she was glad I had met our son. She looked just as I remembered her. Still so beautiful. I could smell the scent of roses as she faded into the mist. I caught a glimpse of Rachael behind her. How is that possible?" He finished with a catch in his voice.

"Mother and Eagle Talon had many spirit beings around them. I've felt her every day since I finally gave in to my grief, and she has led me here to meet you. Perhaps it is to heal your body and heal your sadness as well. You have helped me with my grief in the short time I have been with you. I would enjoy hearing stories about Mother when you want to talk about her."

"I do, and we will talk soon. But right now, I'm hungry."

Later that day, Will was preparing to replace the first maggots with new ones. As he was picking them out, his fingers touched an object, and Jim jumped. "Hey, that hurt."

"Mary Lee, please get your tweezers and put them in boiling water before you bring them to me. There is something in the wound that needs to be removed."

James, Jim's five-year-old son, had been watching from the doorway. "May I come in, sir, and watch what he is doing to your leg?" he asked hopefully.

"If it is all right with Will, it's fine with me."

"Sure, I would appreciate the help."

James came flying across the room, leaping up on the bed to stare at the hole in his father's leg with the wriggling white maggots in it.

"Can't believe they are not eating his leg off," James said in awe.

"They eat only the bad flesh that is making him sick, James," Will replied.

Mary Lee soon returned with the tweezers in a bowl of boiling water. Will carefully removed the maggots and shifted the pus around with the tweezers until he could see an object deep in the wound. Grasping the tip of it, he tried to remove it, but it did not come out easily.

Jim felt the movement, which caused him pain. Will gripped it tighter, pulling it out with a little force.

"Oh, that hurts," yelled Jim.

Holding the tweezers up, Will showed them a two-inch sliver of bone that had been shaved off when the bullet passed through Jim's leg. It had continued to irritate the injury, not allowing it to heal.

"Can I help you put the worms back in the hole?"

"Yes, James, we will use the tweezers because it makes it much easier to grab them. Don't you think?"

Breathless, James was awed by what Will was doing. Just before he finished, Will handed James the tweezers and pointed at the remaining maggots in the jar. "Can you pick them up and place them here in the wound?"

James took the tweezers and, directed by Will, placed the remaining maggots in the gaping hole in his father's leg. Will then bandaged the wound.

"You did very well, James. Thank you for wanting to help your father."

"Isn't he your father, too? That's what the other kids are saying."

Both young men turned to look at their elder. Silence echoed in the room before Jim said to his youngest son, "Yes, he is my oldest son, as you are my youngest. That makes you both very special to me. James, will you tell Will what your name is?"

"James William McKenna! But everyone calls me James," he said proudly.

"Will, tell James what your name is."

"Well, James, my name is James William McKenna, and everyone calls me Will."

"But how can we have the same name?" James asked in confusion.

"I have been thinking about that, James, and I think we need to make a few small changes to both your names. How about calling Will James William McKenna II and you James William McKenna III...since you are the youngest? Would that work out OK?"

James was silent for a while as he considered what his father had said. A smile broke out on his face as he said, "I think that is a wonderful idea because we will have the same name as our father! Do you like that, Will?"

"Yes, I do very much." His voice broke before he could gain control of his emotions.

"Now that we have gotten the bone out, you will heal, Jim. I'll get Mary Lee to bring you another cup of the herbal tea. You need to sleep now."

12

Eli

When Rowdy and Eli returned to the ranch, it was afternoon and very hot. Rowdy's head was hurting again, and he was feeling sick to his stomach. All he wanted to do was lie down when he got back.

"Rowdy, I have Indian medicines and healing teas that might help your head. Would you like to try them when we get back up to the ranch house?"

"Eli, as sick as I get with my head hurting, I am willing to try anything if you think it will help."

Hannah met them at the front door. "Father, the horses in the back pasture have broken out and scattered. I want to take the hands from the fence building and leave right away to trail them."

"Hannah, after Eli fixes me some of his Indian medicines, take him to Shorty and let Eli do it so he will become familiar with the ranch. I want them to learn to work together. But right now, I need to lie down," Rowdy said from the hallway as he continued down toward his room.

Eli turned toward the kitchen to brew Rowdy the tea for his headache.

Hannah was livid. She followed him into the kitchen before she spewed her anger. "You may be Father's bastard son, but you will never own this ranch. It belongs to me." Whirling, she left the house, slamming the door as she headed for the barn.

An emotion Eli had never experienced before shook him to his core. Hannah's sudden and unexpected attack sent a rush of adrenaline to his head, making him dizzy and sick to his stomach in an instant. He stood quietly, watching the water come to a boil as he tried to rein his emotions back under control.

Taking a cup from the cabinet, he poured boiling water over the herbs as he stirred with a spoon, continuing to contemplate Hannah's accusation. Her reaction to Rowdy's request overwhelmed him.

After knocking on the door of Rowdy and Ruth's bedroom, he waited until he heard a weak "come in" from the interior.

Rowdy had been lying down but sat up as Eli entered with the tea.

"Drink this and you will sleep. I hope it will relieve the pain also. Talk with you later."

Rowdy sipped at the hot brew as Eli left, closing the door quietly behind him. Still trying to decide what to do, he left the house and walked toward the river.

Ruth had observed Hannah's outburst and completely understood her daughter's reaction. In the last few days, their world had been turned upside down with the revelation of a love child from Rowdy's past. She felt as helpless as Hannah. Rowdy had been honest with her from the start about his past and his love for Laura. Her rejection had devastated him. Ruth had been there to pick up the pieces and create a life with this wonderful man.

At first, she had encouraged Rowdy to get to know Eli, but now she worried about what would happen to the world they had made together. Going into the kitchen, she began kneading the bread dough in preparation for tonight's supper as her mind wandered to what-ifs.

Hours later Hannah and the ranch hands returned with the missing horses. Putting them in the corral, she wanted a look at the deep gashes on several of them. After catching them, she washed the wounds, putting medicine on each cut while Shorty held them. They recognized the deep cuts had been made by a mountain lion.

"No wonder they spooked, Shorty; they were attacked by a mountain lion. We will go out tomorrow and track it before it can kill any of the horses. It almost got several of these."

"Yes, ma'am. We need to find it before it does any harm to the colts," replied Shorty.

After making plans for an early start the next morning, Hannah headed to the house to wash up for supper. Her mother glanced behind her as she ran into the kitchen, asking, "Where's Eli? Didn't he go with you?"

"No, haven't seen him," she replied and ignored the looks her mother gave her.

"Oh, I thought he went with you to round up the horses."

"Supper sure smells good. I'll set the table while everyone washes up."

When the family assembled around the table for the evening meal, Rowdy was feeling better.

"Where's Eli?" asked Rowdy.

Daniel, Rowdy's ten-year-old, answered, "I rang the dinner bell for everyone to come to supper. He hasn't shown up yet."

David, the eldest boy, replied, "I saw him saddle his horse and ride out midafternoon."

"Why did he leave? I thought he was helping you with rounding up the horses." Rowdy looked at Hannah.

Stuttering a little, Hannah replied, "Well, uh, he didn't. Shorty and I discovered after we got the horses corralled a mountain lion had attacked them, causing them to scatter. So we plan to leave early tomorrow to track it."

"Hannah, when you talk like that, I know you caused trouble. What did you do?"

"I don't know what you mean. You told us all to hunt the horses, and we did. Whatever Eli decided to do was no concern of mine."

Rowdy eyed his daughter suspiciously before offering the blessing for the meal. Talk about the mountain lion circled the table, but Rowdy's thoughts were on Eli and his whereabouts.

— ~ —

When Eli left the ranch house, he walked in the direction of the river. Deep in thought, he had not noticed where he was going until he tripped over a root and nearly toppled into the river. Sitting down on a log near the peaceful riverbank, he continued to consider all that had happened to him since his mother had died.

After a while, he stood up and walked back in the direction he had come. He went to the barn, saddled his horse, and rode back to the hotel. He did not want to be a bother to anyone here. Perhaps in a few days, he would ride out to see Will and find out how his father was doing...

Two days later, a knock sounded on Eli's hotel door. When he opened the door, Rowdy, with his hat in his hands, looked at him.

"Eli, I am so sorry about what happened. May I come in?"

Eli gestured for Rowdy to enter.

"Please hear me out before you say anything. I found out the cruel things Hannah said to you. She will apologize to you. And I—"

Eli raised his hand to silence Rowdy as he said, "That's not necessary. She was right. I am a bastard. My mother and father were not married. It was a shock to me to realize that. I remembered something Mother wrote in her journal. She said she would make sure no one ever knew Abner Brown was not our father. She didn't want us to live in shame with her sin. Will and I rushed here to find out about our fathers for our sakes, never realizing what the effect would be on your present families. For that I am sorry. I know I have upset your home." He turned toward the window so Rowdy would not see his sadness.

"Please, son, you must listen to me. I am so glad you came. It was sinful what Jim and I did to you and Will, but let us make it right. We want you to come back to the ranch and stay with us like we planned. All of us need to become better acquainted with you."

Eli turned from the window as he said, "I want you and Hannah to know I have a large ranch in the Rockies that I will return to. I do not want anything that belongs to you or her."

"I understand, but please come back."

"I would like to go out to the McKennas' ranch and check on Jim and Will, if you don't mind. I will come out to your ranch during the day, but I will return here at night."

"I know you are hurt by the rejection, but as you become more acquainted with Hannah, you will see her fiery ways and learn to use them to your advantage. Are you ready to go?"

As they left the hotel, Captain Jones greeted them.

"Hello, Rowdy and Eli. I was just coming to talk with you about something I found out about Emily Rose."

"Please tell me you have found her alive!" yelled Rowdy in his fear and excitement.

"I have a bit of information about where she may have been taken. Will you both come over to my office so we can talk more privately?"

Anxious to hear more details, Rowdy led the way to Captain Jones's office. Frank passed out mugs filled with steaming coffee as he motioned for them to sit down in the chairs in front of his desk.

"We captured a desperado who rode with the gang that attacked you. He would not talk at first, but with a little persuasion and a rattlesnake, he told all."

"You tortured him? Is he dead?" asked a stunned Eli.

"Uh, no. We just scared the hell out of him until he told us what we wanted to know. He's over in a jail cell at the sheriff's."

"What did he tell you?" Rowdy asked anxiously.

"A few days ago, I talked with Jim, and he remembered someone saying the name Blackjack. So I put out feelers and was rewarded with someone coming forward about this man. We caught him yesterday, and he told us everything he knew—which wasn't much, but it was more than we had."

"Details, Frank, please," whispered Rowdy. "Is she alive or not?"

"Blackjack Ketchum wanted you and Jim dead. He had told some of the wild ones he would reward them for killing you both. When they failed to kill you, and only took a crazy girl in the raid, he was livid and shot up the bunch. This one got away. As far as he knows about the woman, she was traded to a small band of Apaches who had come up from the border before Blackjack shot the gang. They had been in a place called Tres Jacales. It means Three Huts and is on an island in the middle of the Rio Grande. It's not part of the United States or Mexico. The outlaws flock to it. It has become a no-man's-land."

"So you are saying Emily Rose was traded to a band of Apaches? Oh my God, where is she now?" Rowdy cried, putting his face in his hands. Eli moved closer, placing his arm around his father's shoulders.

"We will leave tomorrow to go there and nose around to find out for sure who the Indians were and where they might be going."

"Will and I want to go with you, Captain Jones," Eli said softly, surprised at his sudden feelings for a girl he had never met. "We want to help get my sister back if we can."

"Sorry, Eli, I will send only Rangers."

"Then you can swear us in before we go!"

Captain Jones looked from Eli to Rowdy, who was staring at his newfound son in admiration.

They left shortly, heading to the Forever Ranch to break the news to Will that he was going to be a Texas Ranger.

13

Will

Will had also been receiving rejection and snide remarks from Jim's children. The children were grieving for their mother, and now they suddenly had a new member of the family who came from a different woman. They were confused and angry. He could feel their deep resentment.

As Will entered the kitchen early on the second morning, he looked around for Mary Lee as he asked Susan, "Is breakfast ready?"

He received a dirty look from Susan, who replied, "Am I supposed to wait on you, too?"

"I'm sorry. What did I do?"

"Mary Lee has a sick husband today, and I have to cook breakfast and take care of everything. And now you are making demands."

"Whoa, Susan. I am not here to cause any kind of trouble for you or your family. I do know how to cook, and I will be happy to help you prepare breakfast. What do you want done?"

Susan stared at her new brother, who had taken the wind out of her thunderstorm by his kindness. She wanted to vent on him, but how could she do that when he was so willing to help?

"Thanks, I will make the biscuits if you will get the bacon frying."

"I can do that."

While they worked together, a peace settled over them. "I am sorry about the loss of your mother. I lost mine last year, and I was devastated. I didn't know how to go on without her. I tried to hide from my grief, but it would not let me."

Susan looked at him with new respect as he continued to talk about his grief.

"Recently, I went into her cabin and discovered her journals. That information has led me here. I came only to find out who I am and what kind of man I came from. Nothing more."

"Thank you for being honest. I have been at a loss since Mother died. It was awful. She was killed in front of all of us. My cousin and best friend, Emily Rose, was taken. Father and Rowdy were shot. Father did not want to live anymore without Mother. I thought I might lose him, too. Thank you for helping him to heal with your Indian medicine. I will always be grateful to you for saving him. Perhaps your coming at this time has given him the will to want to live again."

"I have begun to understand your darkest times may seem to be the end of your world, but then a tiny ray of light appears, and you are led forward. Helping you and your family heal from your grief has helped me as well."

Before long, they called their siblings to breakfast. James chatted on about their new names and how he had helped Will put maggots in Father's leg.

Susan grimaced and shivered, but her younger brothers were awe-struck about how the maggots ate pus. Will joined into the table conversation, and for the first time, he had a sense of belonging.

Later that day, Jim and Will were sitting on the front porch, trying to catch a cool breeze, which was impossible in the afternoon heat in Texas. But at least Jim was up, dressed, and feeling better.

As the trio rode up, their faces displayed surprise at seeing him dressed and sitting on the front porch.

Rowdy was the first one off his horse to grab Jim's hand and slap him on the back as he said, "I am so glad to see you up and about. It seems the maggots feed well on you."

Everyone laughed.

Jim greeted Captain Jones and Eli with strong handshakes as Captain Jones remarked, "The last time I saw you, you didn't look so good, but that was before the boy here showed up and made you want to live again."

Jim chuckled in agreement and invited everyone into the living room as he yelled at Susan to bring refreshments. "It's getting too damn hot to sit out here. Come on in. Will, help me stand up please."

Will assisted his father to stand. Using his cane to gain his balance, Jim walked cautiously into the front room. The coolness of the leather felt good to him as Will eased him into his chair.

Rowdy was quick to tell Jim the news about Emily Rose, although he didn't know much more than that.

"Some of the Rangers are riding out tomorrow for Presidio. I want to go, but I know I am still not able because of my head wound. Sometimes the headaches come on me so quickly I can't see and have to lie down or pass out."

Will spoke up. "Rowdy, I have some Indian herbs that might help you with the headaches."

"Eli has already taken care of me with the herbs. But thanks for offering. It sure helped the other day when I was down again with a bad one."

"When Will removed the maggots, he began filling the wound with healing herbs, and it has begun to draw more of the poison out of my wound. These boys know what they are doing."

"Maggots?" asked Captain Jones as he looked from Jim to Will.

"I'll tell you sometime about his Indians ways and medicines." Jim laughed.

"I have something to ask Will. Since both of your fathers are out of commission, I am short two Rangers. Eli has volunteered to go on tomorrow's trek down near the Rio Grande, but he can't go with the

Rangers unless he is a Texas Ranger. It will be a hard, fast trip. I can make you a Ranger right along with him. Do you want to go also?" asked Captain Jones.

Without hesitation, Will answered, "Yes, sir. I want to help Eli find his sister."

"I was hoping you would say that. Both of you raise your right hands and repeat after me."

Jim and his children, along with Rowdy, looked on proudly as Will and Eli were sworn in. When Captain Jones completed the impromptu ceremony, he handed each man a badge, stating, "These badges were made and designed by Texas Rangers. They are made from Mexican *cinco pesos* cut out in the center to form the Lone Star of Texas, and the words 'Texas Ranger' are inscribed around the star. Wear it proudly."

Susan stepped forward, taking the badge from Eli's warm hand. At her touch, a charge of energy, lightning, or magic swept through both their bodies. Blue eyes locked with green eyes as the spell enveloped them as if they were the only ones in the room. Pinning the Ranger star to his shirt pocket, she quietly said, "Just because you are a Texas Ranger now doesn't mean you go get yourself shot. Please come back safely."

Eli blinked several times and licked his suddenly dry lips as he looked down at this beautiful, dark-haired young woman. Her cheeks turned rosy at her boldness and moisture formed in her eyes because he might be in danger, but he liked what her eyes were telling him. Promises of a tomorrow? With her? Taking her hand, he held it for a few seconds before she pulled away.

14

Emily Rose

Kidnapped!

Emily Rose Adams couldn't believe she had been kidnapped from her front yard surrounded by her family and friends. Since then, when she managed a few hours of sleep, she still heard the explosions of the handguns and rifles as the outlaws fired on the happy Easter group. She heard the screams from the horses as they reared up in fear as well as her own cries as she saw Jim fall from his horse and his wife, Rachael, shot between the eyes, tumbling headfirst from the wagon.

Nothing would ever remove the acrid smell of gunpowder, the dust from the horses' hooves, and the coppery scent of fresh blood, which hung in her mind like spirits rising from their graves, from her nostrils. How do you ever forget such a terrible day? And then she had been taken from her loved ones as easily as one picked a flower from a bush.

Emily Rose became conscious of the sounds of a crackling fire and a cool, gentle wind blowing through the trees.

Fear raced through her body. She remembered. The outlaws had killed her father before her very eyes. Taking several deep breaths to keep from crying out, she glanced around to see if anyone was up. Only one man sat by the fire, making coffee.

The outlaws knew the Texas Rangers would be on their trail, so they had ridden hard for the Mexico border. But for some unknown reason, they had turned west instead of continuing south. Why?

Most of the outlaws were Mexican, but several who appeared to be the leaders were white. She overheard them on a number of occasions talking about someone named Blackjack and how happy he would be to learn they had killed the two Rangers.

Emily Rose squeezed her eyes shut as she remembered seeing Jim shot first, falling from his horse before they shot her father. She watched as the nightmare played out over and over in her memories, as her father reeled backward when the bullet hit him in the head and bright-red blood spattered against the white wall of their home as his limp body slumped down to the porch.

A dark-brown arm had grabbed her from her yard, lifting her onto his horse as they rode out. As she yelled and fought to break free, the kidnapper slammed his fist into her face, and everything went black.

When she came to, one of the white men had questioned her, asking her who she was. Too afraid to tell him she was Rowdy Adams's daughter, she faked answering by saying, "I'm not sure. My mind is so fuzzy. Where am I? I don't know this place. I don't know who you are. Oh, look, it's a pretty butterfly." She reached out to touch an imaginary creature.

The men draw back as if afraid. Seeing their reaction, she sensed they were frightened of crazy people. Hoping to use it to her advantage to stay alive, she shouted, "I'm hungry!" and began to dance around in circles. Several of the men wearing Mexican sombreros ran into one another as they hurried to find her something to eat.

Emily Rose knew her charade might help keep her alive if they didn't know who she was. So she continued to do unexpected things to keep up her act. The best one so far had happened about a week after she had been kidnapped. She woke the camp in the middle of the night as she stood up, singing "Onward, Christian Soldiers" as she marched around.

The outlaws had leaped to their feet with guns drawn and pointed at her. She raised her arms toward the stars, sunk to her pallet, and pulled her blanket over her head to keep them from seeing her laughter. From the whispered excitement, she knew she had scared them again and hoped this would keep them away from her.

Unknown to her kidnappers, she was fluent in Spanish as well as French. She had grown up on the ranch where her father worked with Mexican vaqueros. They'd taught her and her brothers Spanish. When she was sixteen, her parents had sent her off to finishing school for two years, where she had learned French. She had returned home recently.

She listened to the men talking in Spanish. They were trying to decide what to do with her, short of killing her. They did not want to kill a crazy person because they truly feared what would happen to them in the afterlife. That was funny to her because they were bad outlaws and worried about the afterlife. But their fear was keeping her alive for now.

At times it was difficult to keep from blushing when they used vulgar words and profanity in their conversations. She tried to keep from laughing when they called one another names like *pendejo* or *pinche idiota*.

She was forced to ride double because they did not have a horse for her. Each day she rode behind a different one. They traveled fast and did not want to wear out their horses with an extra burden. She did not like being close to any of them because they smelled of strong cigarettes, rotten teeth, and unwashed bodies.

Of course, she smelled bad too by now. But that was in her favor, she hoped. Because she had to hug them around the waist to hold on, and her large breasts pressed against their backs, she heard several comments in Spanish about her breasts.

On those occasions, she would have one of her crazy fits, giving them a good scare, and nobody wanted her to ride with him the next day. They had begun to call her "loco woman" or "*Cochina* woman," which pleased her. It proved she was convincing them she was crazy, and she was stinking.

Emily Rose was fair skinned and suffered from the burning Texas sun. They had been on the run for several days when she remembered one of the Mexican vaqueros at her ranch telling her what to do if she should ever begin to sunburn. She had laughed at him, telling him she would never do that. But now she decided was the perfect time to try it out.

Picking up a freshly dropped horse biscuit, she spread the manure over her sun-blistered arms. The relief from the burn was instant as she wiped the biscuit along her arms. She was glad her face had not burned because she did not want to smear this on her face so close to her nose. She was thankful for small blessings: her Easter bonnet had been securely tied under her chin, and she had not lost it in the fracas when she was abducted.

Now no one wanted her to ride behind them because of the horse shit on her arms and her weird actions. They soon began to make her ride behind each of the men only a few hours at a time.

Today they came upon a small band of Mescalero Apaches. It was apparent some of the Mexican men knew the leader, Yellow Knife.

Yellow Knife had told them in Spanish they were near the Fort McKavett army post, and they had managed to slip away from the soldiers. Before long a bottle of tequila was bought out and passed around. The drinking and bragging began.

One of the outlaws secured Emily Rose to a tree and told her not to act crazy or else she would be sorry. She watched uneasily as the men got drunker and louder.

Glances in her direction from the outlaws as well as the Apaches started her heart pounding for her safety. Just before dark, a fierce-looking Apache untied her, roughly shook her, and dragged her over to a horse. She stared hatefully at the outlaws as she was placed on an Indian pony and led away.

The drunken fools had traded her to Indians! What was she to do now?

As there was only an Indian blanket over the horse's back, Emily Rose had to grip the horse's long mane to stay on. Thankful she was a good rider, she kept her balance by using her leg strength as she tightened her hold on the horse's sides.

Hours later they stopped, built a small fire, wrapped up in their blankets, and went to sleep. She had been tied to a small bush and given no food or water, and a guard had been posted to watch her and the camp while the others slept.

Traveling with the outlaws, she had been aware of the direction they were going, but since the Indians had moved in the darkness, she did not know where she was. She felt a sense of hopelessness for the first time since she had been kidnapped. She hoped when the sun came up she would be able to get an idea as to where she was.

Kicked awake by a moccasined foot, she was shaken roughly again as she was pushed up on the horse.

"Please, I need water," she begged.

The Apaches ignored her and set a hard pace toward the mountains in the distance. The sun was at her back today, and she knew the direction they traveled. But as the sun rose higher and beamed down on her, she suffered from the intense heat and lack of water.

Just before she passed out and fell off her horse, the band stopped at a tiny spring bubbling up between two rocks. After the men had drunk their fill, she was led to the spring. The pool filled gradually, but as it seeped into the shallow rock bowl, she was able to splash cold water on her face as she revived. She sighed at the pleasure it gave her. As soon as she had quenched her thirst, her stomach rumbled loudly enough that her captors heard it and laughed.

"Please, do you have food?" she pleaded in English.

One of them tossed her a strip of jerky, and she nodded her thanks at him before lowering her eyes. She remembered reading somewhere not to look an Indian directly in the eyes. Why? She couldn't remember the reason.

Chewing the dried meat, she hoped it was not dog. She had heard stories of the Indians starving and having to eat their dogs. She looked down at her Easter dress to move her mind away from the meat she was enjoying. Her mother had made it especially for her return home from school.

Now that happy Easter Sunday morning seemed so long ago. Her pink-dotted cotton dress was no longer pink. Instead it had green grass

stains smeared with dirt from sleeping on the hard ground, horse manure, and blood from when the outlaw had struck her, cutting her lip.
The blood was no longer red but a faded brown. The hem had ripped out
and hung uneven in places. Her white, long-legged bloomers were no
longer white. They were filthy from riding horseback. They had become
her buffer for her legs and the sweaty, hairy, and bony back of the pony
she rode.

She was thankful she had not been raped or killed by the outlaws and
now this band of Indians. She still acted crazy at times, causing them to
keep their distance. Where they were taking her and what would happen
to her she did not know. Unable to understand their words and grunts,
she was fearful for her life.

At times when the band stopped to rest, Emily Rose was allowed to
move around the camp and pick up sticks for the fire.

As she did so, she watched for plants she was familiar with. She had
decided she would poison the Indians if she ever got the chance, so she
had to be ready. Today she had been able to grab stinkweed and tuck
it into her pocket. If eaten, it would cause a stomach upset and lots of
vomiting. She gathered different seeds and leaves that were available.
She also had discovered sage leaves. When dried, they were good for
seasoning meat.

The Indians soon mounted up, and the leader motioned for her to
get on her horse. After leading him over to a small boulder, she was able
to climb onto the horse unaided by any of them.

The leader nodded and grunted at her. She was not sure if that was a
good thing or not.

Many more long, hot days followed that one pleasant stop. They ate
little and traveled much. One night as the men sat around the small
campfire, she overhead one speaking to the others in Spanish. He
was telling the group they had to watch out for the soldiers from Fort
Stockton. They had gotten near one of their units today. He had seen
signs of soldiers that were only a few hours old.

Her heart sang with excitement. She now had an idea of where she
was in Texas. There were soldiers nearby. She wanted to slip away, but

how could she? She was bound with rawhide and tied to a thorny mesquite bush.

She had watched for weeks for a chance to escape, but it never came. Perhaps now she should begin to plan on "what if" should happen.

Awakened before daylight, she began her long day again. She looked at the Indian who had spoken Spanish. On closer inspection, she saw he was Mexican, riding with the Indians. He smiled at her, showing missing and blackened teeth. She turned away, not wanting to encourage him. She had to act soon. She could not continue to travel with the warriors.

Three days later, the terrain changed as they moved away from the flat, arid areas of west Texas and into a mountainous area. Tall pines offered her a reprieve from the terrible baking sun and heat. The lower temperatures were refreshing. She inhaled the pine-scented air, enjoying the pleasant sensation.

Finding a circle of boulders high up the mountainside, the Apaches stopped to make camp. Soon one of the warriors returned with several turkeys. Someone grabbed Emily Rose, pushing her toward the dead birds, indicating with grunts and pointing that she was to prepare them. They had not wanted her to cook for them before.

"I will need a knife to gut them," she said as she looked up at the fearsome group. The Mexican pulled a small knife from his leggings and threw it at her. She screamed as the knife sailed passed her head, jabbing into the tree behind her.

Laughter from the group exploded as they enjoyed her terror.

Lowering her head, she removed the feathers from the birds. She heard the sounds of a small stream nearby. Taking the birds and the knife to the stream, she washed and finished preparing them for roasting. Someone brought her a handful of wild onions, a small sack of salt, and two green pine branches to skewer the birds on.

Looking around to see if her captors were watching her, she took from her left pocket dried weeds and seeds she had been collecting. She knew enough to know what was good to eat and what was not. Among the plants she had saved were stinkweed and sage, and she crumbled these together. Hoping the strong sage flavor would cover up the stinkweed taste, she rubbed her mixture inside and out of the birds, adding lots of salt, hoping the saltiness would cover up the special blend she had rubbed on one of the birds.

She notched one of the sticks to mark the one she would eat from. After putting half the wild onions with green tops in each bird, she pushed the pointed ends into each bird.

In her other pocket, she had mixed sage and other plants that were edible. She planned to cook the poisoned turkey first and the other a little later. The warriors always ate first before giving her any food.

As expected, when the first turkey came off the fire, the Indians divided it between them. She was relieved to see that each one got a large hunk of it and ate the cooked wild onions, too. When the other one came off, they did the same thing but, at the last minute, threw her the back.

She ate it with relish, having smelled the roasting meat as it cooked. The turkey was delicious, and only the bones were left. Cleanup was an easy task before she was tied again to a tree as the camp settled down.

Hours later, the sounds of someone close by retching and moaning woke Emily Rose. Before long, the camp came to life with the warriors puking and running for the nearby bushes. The herbs were working!

Glancing around to see if anyone was watching her, she wiggled around until she could pull her skirt up to reach her pocket, where she had hidden the small knife. After easing it from her skirt pocket, she cut the rawhide bindings. The warrior who had been sleeping nearest her had suddenly leaped up, leaving all his possessions.

Picking up her blanket, she moved in the darkness toward his pallet. She found his rifle, a beaded bag with jerky, and his blanket. Grabbing everything, she tucked the rifle into the folds of her skirt before slipping away into the underbrush with his multicolored Indian blanket about her shoulders.

The horses had been hobbled behind her on a grassy plain. She knew the one she wanted.

Emily Rose eased up to the leader's black stallion with the white blaze and threw her blanket over his back. After unfastening the hobbles, she grabbed a handful of coarse mane hair and swung up on his back. Clicking softly to him, she guided him away from the camp. Knowing they would follow her when they discovered she was gone, she galloped away when she was certain she would not be heard.

15

Black Hawk

Black Hawk's heart had been heavy since he had kissed his sister, Raven, goodbye on their family ranch high in the Colorado Rockies weeks ago. He smiled as he remembered discovering Raven in Wyoming when she should have been in Washington. What an adventure she had had. Perhaps she'd experienced her first love. But she was happy to be recused and joyfully returned to their ranch.

After finding the letters from their mother and reading her journals, they had been able to share their grief with each other. It had been a time for each of them to help the other grow stronger in their understanding of what had happened. Their brothers' sudden exit had been explained after they had read Mother's journals.

He had wanted to remain, but his dreams and visions had forced him to leave Raven and his home to seek them out. He had many questions about the visions, but the answers were hidden from him. All he knew was a powerful driving force was causing him to seek out a white mountain with a black river flowing below it and a red rose dripping blood. He was a powerful medicine man, but even he did not understand what any of the visions meant. All he could do was follow where he was led. There was a reason. Was it for the tribe or a personal journey he had to make for himself? He did not know.

Today when he awoke, Silver was watching him from the edge of the trees. He had not seen him since his mother had passed. What did it mean? The wolf turned and trotted back into the cover of the trees.

After seeing Silver, he broke camp without eating breakfast, sensing it was a sign he was nearing his destination. He munched on dried corn and jerky as he rode Powder onward. Later in the morning, he saw a tee-pee set up near a spring in the distance. An old Indian man sat crossed-legged before a small fire as he roasted a rabbit on a spit.

The aged man had long silver hair streaming about him as he sat wrapped in a ragged blanket. A beaded headband kept his hair from falling into his face as a strong south wind blew his hair up in the back, making him look as if long spikes extended from his head. His face had deep creases carved into the dark-red skin from the ravages of life and time. "Tanned like leather" was a whisper through Black Hawk's mind. The elder's battle-scarred war shield was attached to the old warrior's war lance as it leaned against the teepee. Many eagle feathers tied to the lance moved in the morning breeze. It held many victories.

"Ho!" The elder raised his skinny arm as he called out to Black Hawk as he rode up.

"Ho!" Black Hawk returned the greeting.

"I have been waiting for you, Black Hawk," he acknowledged in an ancient language.

Black Hawk was surprised he understood the ancient words, having never heard them before.

"How do I understand you, O Ancient One?" he asked.

"Black Hawk, there are many things you don't know you know," he answered with a cackle as he showed his toothless mouth and his sky-blue eyes met Black Hawk's sapphire ones.

Black Hawk slid off his stallion and sat down by the small campfire on the well-worn Indian blanket the old tribal elder motioned to.

"Ancient One, you know my name. May I ask yours?"

He cackled again, saying, "You know me, but you don't know me! You may call me Sinapu."

"Sinapu means 'wolf' in our tongue. I am happy to visit with you today."

"The food is ready to eat now. Let us give thanks to the Great Spirit for providing us food for our bellies and the rabbit spirit for his sacrifice." He grinned as he sang a song of praise to the Great Spirit.

After they had eaten, Sinapu began. "I am here to complete your teachings from your father. He died before he had fully instructed you in shifting." He watched Black Hawk's face to see his reaction.

A stunned silence followed the statement as the words sank in. "My father has sent you? You have talked with him?"

"Yes. We have talked many times. He is well and happy now that your mother has joined him. He wanted you to be taught by a tribal elder to use your natural forces for good and to understand about shifters and to know it has passed to your sister as well. It is rare for siblings to share the same power. Many times both will have other ways to show their spiritual power. But you both share the same strong powers."

"What spiritual powers do we share? I did not know she had powers. What is a shifter?"

"Black Hawk, do you not remember being in your hawk form? It has only happened a few times. Once when you found your sister by a river and made her leave with you."

"I...uh...thought that had been a dream. I did not know I had changed to an animal," he stammered and stuttered.

"You cannot shift into an animal but into a winged bird. Your power is strongest as a hawk. Your name tells your totem powers. Your sister's name is Raven, meaning her powers come from her totem, the raven."

Black Hawk stood up, unable to sit any longer as he paced before the elder and considered what the elder had told him.

Sinapu sat quietly as he sipped a special tea he had brewed from white willow bark.

Black Hawk turned to Sinapu, asking, "Will you teach me more of this power? I still do not understand."

Sinapu nodded and began to tell Black Hawk about shifters.

"Our totems are many. Some have the mighty animal powers. Others have the bird or winged shifter power. But others can shift into any being or animal they desire. The power in your family has been the winged creatures. Your father was an eagle, but you are a black hawk. It is a strong power when used for good. But it can be used for evil. You must choose wisely when to use it and whom you allow to know your power."

"Does my sister know of her special powers?"

"No. She has changed several times but hides her memories from herself. It has frightened her because she has not been taught how to use these powers. But she will soon begin her training as well. You must learn to use your powers for good. Evil surrounds us, Black Hawk. You alone must choose which power will rule you. Are you willing to complete your training?"

Black Hawk paced for a while longer before settling again on the old Indian's blanket as he said, "Sinapu, I am ready to learn."

"Give your heart over to the Great Spirit and we will begin your training. After you learn to control your power, then you will continue your journey on your vision quest." Sinapu smiled as he chanted a cleansing song for Black Hawk.

Several days later, Black Hawk awoke wrapped in his blanket. He was warm and comfortable and did not want to stir. He became aware of the sounds of the wind blowing through the short shrub brush, the happy noise of the birds singing their morning songs in the tall tree, and the water in the creek splashing over rocks as it went on its own journey. He felt he was alone.

Opening his eyes, he looked up at the bright morning sky. The sun had been up for hours! He leaped up, calling to Sinapu for letting him sleep so late.

The silence that followed was chilling. Black Hawk turned completely around as he surveyed the campsite—or lack of one. There was no teepee, no old elder, not even a campfire!

Was he crazy? Had he run a high fever and hallucinated Sinapu teaching him? The ancient was gone without a trace!

He squatted, placing his head in his hands as he fought for control. He was sane. He was a medicine man. He was a hawk.

As he thought about being a hawk, his body responded. Spreading his arms out from his body, he felt no pain as black feathers appeared along his arms, which became wings, and the rest of his body followed the transformation within seconds. He ruffled his feathers and looked down at his yellow talon feet. Hopping over to a pool of still water, he looked at his reflection. Shocked. Surprised. Pleased. These were all emotions careening throughout his feathered body. Yes, it was true. He was a shifter. He had not only dreamed it.

Flapping his arms—wings—he rose upward into the sky. Air currents took him higher than he had ever been before. Fear rose up, causing bile in his bird throat before he remembered what Sinapu had taught him. Then he relaxed and enjoyed the sensations breaking over the flap of his wings. Strange emotions filled his thoughts as he circled above the deserted campsite. He could see Powder hobbled and grazing below him. His eyes were keen and sharp; he saw mice and rabbits scurrying for cover as he flew over them.

Black Hawk wanted to stay like this longer, but he remembered he must return to his human form and continue his journey. Thinking about returning to human form while he was airborne was not a good idea.

Suddenly, he spiraled downward, managing to crash-land in the creek in his human form.

Well, I better do more practicing before I try to show off, he thought.

He laughed out loud as he waded out of the flowing creek, but he sank back into the water, deciding he needed a bath before he continued onward. His clothes had returned to his body as he had changed. Strange. No, it was magic, he decided. Powerful magic.

An hour later, he was refreshed, having bathed, then eaten jerky, and now he was riding Powder toward the distant snow-topped mountains.

As the mountains grew closer, he remembered what Sinapu had told him of the Great Spirit creating the world in the sacred mountains of the Sierra Blanca, Guadalupe, Three Sisters, and the Oscura Mountain Peak—all powerful, magical mountains of New Mexico.

When Black Hawk had asked about the White Mountain and his vision quest, Sinapu had refused to say more except, "You will know when you find it."

Perhaps this is why I have been brought here, Black Hawk thought.

Riding up on a high ridge several days later, he looked down on a sprawling valley. There, spreading from one end of the flat valley to the other, was a massive flowing black river. It had waves, twirls, and high crests. But he sucked in his breath in surprise when he realized the river was silent and still as if frozen in time. A chill ran through him; was it a premonition?

Beyond the black river stood the snow-white mountains he had seen in his dreams. He was here. As he looked in each direction, he saw the surrounding sacred mountains Sinapu had spoken of. Still the question remained: Why had he been brought here? And what did the red rose dripping blood mean?

Nudging Powder down the steep slope toward the river that did not move, he was curious to examine this strange object.

When he reached the edge of black river, he climbed down from his horse to inspect it. Expecting it to be warm, he was surprised when the shiny blackness was as cold as death and solid as a rock. How could it be a river?

Apparently, it had been this way for a long time, since dirt had filled crevices, birds and winds had deposited seeds, and the rains had sprouted the seeds. Now vegetation grew in its nooks and crannies. Cactus, desert grasses, yuccas, and other spiny plants dotted the uneven top. Many of the Great Spirit's beings lived here. He saw horned toads, green lizards, snakes, and giant spider webs spanning between one still wave to another.

He continued to walk, look, and feel the solid formation. Suddenly, he touched space as he discovered an opening to a cave. The entrance was not visible unless you knew where to look. It blended into the blackness. The access was wide enough to allow him to enter.

Inside he felt along the smooth black walls and was amazed at how ice cold it was on such a hot day. The walls were not jagged as other caves he had been in. These were smooth as glass. Water dripped into a small pool near the entrance. Waiting as his eyes grew accustomed to the darkness, he saw the walls begin to sparkle with tiny lights. He felt mystic forces surrounded him.

Sensing this was where he had been led, he followed the long tunnel into the interior of the motionless black river. Amazement grew as he explored the cave, discovering the sunlight from above caused the sparkling lights as they reflected through the black crystal ceiling. The cave's glow enfolded him, and he felt protected and a reverence here. He was able to stand upright, and when he stood on tiptoe, he could touch the ceiling.

The end of the tunnel tapered upward into a small funnel shape, through which he could see blue sky high above. It would work as a chimney for his campfire tonight. He would build his fire here and wait to see why his visions brought him to this powerful place.

Returning to Powder, he pulled his two saddlebags off and removed the Indian blanket he used as a saddle. He led his horse into the cave for water before returning him outside and hobbling him so he could graze peacefully before dark. He would bring him into the cave for the night later.

For now, Black Hawk settled his few items in the cave, dragged wood to the entrance for later, then took his bow and arrows out to hunt for his supper.

When it grew dark, he brought Powder into the cave for protection from predators. After settling his horse, he returned to his campfire to contemplate the night as he sat cross-legged on his blanket. He opened Eagle Talon's beaded buckskin bag given to him when his father died. It was an honor as a chosen son to have his father's medicine bag. It contained his red pipe, his eagle bone whistle, and various rattles for certain rituals and ceremonies.

Tonight Black Hawk chose the eagle bone whistle to begin. He played several songs of praises before chanting as he beat on his small drum. Soon his chanting became prayers to the Great Spirit as he waited.

As his small fire died down, the vision of the snow-white mountains and the Black River appeared before his eyes. Was he awake or dreaming?

Shapes took form, floating down from the sacred mountains and assembling in a semicircle in the black river cave around him.

All the Indian chiefs were adorned in the ceremonial beaded buckskins of their individual tribes. The honored designs designated all nations of the People. Full war bonnets adorned their heads, or single eagle feathers were plaited into their gray and silver hair. The assemblage was impressive.

Black Hawk had grown up hearing about the Council of Ancients but never expected to be honored with a visit from them. Only when a great need arose did they choose someone to receive their message. He acknowledged each one's presence as he bowed his head toward each chief. He was honored but felt so humble before them.

A tall man of great age rose from the center of the assembly. His long hair, as white as the winter snow, flowed down his shoulders to his hips. Three eagle feathers were attached to strands of his hair. His dark and heavily wrinkled face was kindly yet had sternness about it. But his dark eyes held much sadness.

"I am called Grandfather of our people. We are the Council of Ancients, who watch over our land and our Peoples. You were summoned here to fulfill your destiny, Black Hawk."

"I am humbled to be before you and the Ancients. Will you tell me of this amazing place?"

"The Black River came before time began. The Great Spirit spoke, and Mother Earth parted, giving birth to a flowing, red-hot river. As it escaped out of Mother Earth's life-giving body, it began running to the end of the valley as a child wanting to break free of its mother's hold. It did not know what it was to be cold. It had always been held within the protection of Mother Earth. It hurried faster away from her warmth. The mountains blew cold winds, and the snow fell onto it, causing great smoke to rise. As it cooled, the mighty river began to harden and freeze as you see it now."

He continued. "Our people call it the Valley of Fires, for the many fires that burn as they send up smoke signals, begging Mother Earth to return it back into her warmth. This cave was created as it drew its last breath in its death throes before it became cold and still."

"Grandfather, it is truly an amazing place. Thank you for allowing me to be here. I am ready to learn what you want me to do."

"You are descended from great warriors and shamans who came before you. Your father, Eagle Talon, was one and a powerful medicine man of our People. You are of our People, as well as of the white man. It was decided before your birth you would become a servant to our People. But your gift must come willingly from within you. We will guide you if you choose this path. You must decide whether to walk the way of the white man or the way of your People. We know your heart is heavy."

"Yes, it is true. I have not decided what I want to do in this life. I am at a crossroads. I need your help."

"We are always with you, my son. Pray for guidance from your spirit guides. Your journey will not be easy, but you must always follow your heart."

The assembly nodded at Black Hawk as they vanished into a misty smoke.

"Wait! Please tell me what to do!"

But they had disappeared as silently as they had appeared.

Black Hawk jerked awake. He had been dreaming, but he knew it was not a dream. It was a vision telling him he had to decide what to do with his life. An eagle's feather drifted slowly down, landing on his blanket. Picking it up, he knew it was a sign the council had been there and a reminder he was not alone. Pushing the feather into the band around his head, he spent the rest of the night in prayer as they had asked. He prayed to be led in the right direction.

The early-morning sun was peeking over the White Mountains as Black Hawk, deep in thought, rode toward them. He had been brought to this place to meet the Council.

But why here? Couldn't it have been in Colorado instead of New Mexico? Always questions.

Midmorning he heard the soft thuds of water splashing down the mountainside over rocks. Anticipating a cool drink of water, he turned his horse in its direction as he followed an animal trail toward the sounds.

The creek flowed between two large boulders with a narrow trail on the outside edge. The animal trail was wedged between two rocks just large enough for Powder to walk through.

As they came out of the boulders into the sunshine, Powder stopped as he raised his head, sensing something. The glint of sunlight on a metal barrel was Black Hawk's first awareness he was not alone.

When the bullet left the rifle, he saw it coming at him as if in slow motion. Before he could react, it slammed into his head. He felt himself lifted off his horse as he flew backward through the air...and then, all went black.

Black Hawk was again in the white swirling mists he had seen in his dreams. The mist parted as two figures came toward him.

"Mother? Father? You are here. Am I dead?"

His mother's hand soothed his forehand to calm him as she knelt by his side, saying, "You are not dead but badly injured. You are at a crossroads in your life, and when you recover, you will have decisions to make. Sinapu is pulling your healing herbs out of your medicine bag so they can be used to heal you."

Eagle Talon held his son's hand and nodded in agreement as he said, "You will make the right choices, son—when you follow your heart."

With that they were gone, and he felt the loss all over again.

— —

Emily Rose had been on the trail for two days and two long nights since she had escaped the Apaches. She was very tired, very hungry, and very nervous. She had eaten the last of the jerky last night. When she heard the horse's hooves on the rocky trail, she knew they were getting close to catching her.

She had been resting a few minutes in the brush across from the boulders. Holding the rifle against a tree and sighting it on the trail, she waited for the Indians to come around the rocks.

The shot echoed throughout the valley as she watched him fly off his white horse. *White horse?* she thought. *None of the Apaches ride a white horse.*

When she slipped over to where the Indian lay, his horse was standing over him as a large silver wolf appeared. It trotted over to him, licked him on the cheek, and nosed around in the bag at his waist, pulling out several pouches.

It lay one pouch on his chest, then dropped the other into a small medicine cup it had pulled from the pouch also. The wolf looked up at her with its beautiful, gleaming sky-blue eyes, then turned and trotted off the way it had come.

What just happened?

She had seen it but wasn't sure what she saw. But one thing was clear. The Indian was bleeding from a serious head wound—that she had given him.

"Oh, please don't die. I'm sorry I shot you!" she said, wringing her hands, trying to decide what to do first.

16

The Twins

"No! No! No! Don't shoot!" Eli shouted as he roused the Ranger camp.

"What's wrong, Eli?" Will yelled as he shook Eli awake.

"I saw Black Hawk shot. I saw the bullet coming through the air as if I was the target. I felt it as it slammed into my...his head," Eli cried as he covered his face with his hands. "Someone shot our brother," he cried out again, inconsolable.

The other Texas Rangers had gathered around Eli. Captain Jones asked, "Could you recognize where he was? Or who shot him?"

"All I saw was tall pine trees, a rifle, the fire from the muzzle, and the bullet coming right at me...or him. I saw his body fly off his horse, Powder...That's how I knew it was him. What can we do, Will?"

"Since we don't know where he is or even when this happened, all we can do is wait. I know it is hard, but we can pray he is all right."

"Captain Jones, before I saw Black Hawk shot, I was told to warn you about going to Tres Jacales. You are to stay away from there."

"What do you mean, you were told to warn me? By whom?"

"I don't know. This has never happened to me before. Our brother, Black Hawk, has visions, and we know they come true. Our housekeeper, Sadie, and Marty, her sister, do, too. So I would say for you to heed its warning. But I am not going any farther toward the border. I have a great sense of foreboding about going there. I am returning to San Antonio."

"You can't turn back now, since we are so close. You have orders, Ranger."

"Here is my badge. I can no longer go with you. I'm sorry." Saying that, Eli folded up his bedroll and began to saddle his horse.

Captain Jones tried to convince Eli, but Will stepped between them, telling the captain, "Since my brother has resigned, here is my badge as well. We are returning to San Antonio."

Before Captain Jones could argue, the other Rangers started breaking camp to return with the brothers. Captain Jones became angry at the mutiny but finally agreed to return with his men.

After the others had moved away from them, Eli whispered to Will, "I also saw Silver in the dream or vision or whatever the hell it was. It has shaken me up pretty bad."

"I know it has, and I saw Silver the morning I came out of Mother's cabin after I found the letters. So something is going on here, and it looks like you are now getting visions as well. What do you think about that?"

"I can't think right now. All I want to do is get the hell out of here. I can't shake this evil feeling I have about this place up ahead. Let's ride."

17

Emily Rose

When darkness fell, Emily Rose had managed to stop the bleeding by applying cold compresses, had found a more desirable campsite, had dragged the Indian on his blanket to the trees, and had gathered wood and built a fire.

She was exhausted as she rummaged through his saddlebags, thinking they were strange items for an Indian to carry, but in her search, she found rolled white bandages to use for his head wounds instead of strips of her dirty dress. She discovered he also had a change of clothes: a rolled-up cotton shirt and pants.

She was quick to change into them even though they were too big for her. Clean clothes felt heavenly as she turned up the sleeves on the shirt, tied the pants around the waist with a rawhide string, and rolled up the legs so she could walk without falling over.

When she rewrapped his wound, she used the herbs from the pouch the wolf had left on his chest. If the Indian woke up, she would give him some of the herbs brewed in a tea from the other bag. Everything about this handsome man was strange.

In another of the saddlebags, she found parched corn, jerky, flour, sugar, coffee, silverware, a coffeepot, and a frying pan. A coffeepot and a frying pan? *What kind of Indian is he?*

She brewed herself a pot of coffee, leaned back, and enjoyed her first taste of home since she had been kidnapped.

After eating some of his provisions, she placed another log on the fire, wrapped herself in her blanket, and went to sleep.

Unknown to either the injured Indian or the white woman, the blue-eyed silver wolf stood guard.

During the night, the Indian began running a high fever and crying out. Emily Rose was forced to bathe his body with cold spring water after she removed his buckskins. She couldn't keep herself from appraising his strong, powerful arms attached to his rippled, muscular chest. His legs were long and contoured and fit the rest of him quite well. She tried to keep the blanket draped over his man part, but she couldn't keep from acknowledging to herself how well endowed he was.

A strong thought popped into her head, telling her to put cold stones from the stream around him to help lower the fever. *Where did that come from?*

Looking around, Emily Rose saw the silver wolf sitting at the edge of the forest. When she began to pull ice-cold rocks from the water, the wolf moved back into the trees.

She was in awe at how that simple bit of knowledge helped to lower his fever as she continued to bathe his fevered body. She wanted to know more about who or what the silver wolf was. Realizing she had no fear of him surprised her.

Today the Indian moved his arms and legs a little. She had changed the bandage earlier, replacing the bloody herbs with fresh ones. When she raised one of his eyelid, she was startled to see a blue eye.

What kind of Indian is he? she asked herself for the hundredth time. Questions. Questions. No answers.

By nightfall, he was waking up, and his fever was lower. He moaned whenever he moved his head. She asked him several questions but received no acknowledgment. She decided to chatter, hoping he understood some of what she was saying.

"Water. I need water" were his first words as he came out of the fog later that night.

Getting him the small cup, she lifted his head, allowing him to sip the cold spring water.

He choked because his throat was dry but swallowed several mouthfuls before he slipped back into unconsciousness.

When Emily Rose returned from hunting the next morning, she was pleased to see the Indian had turned on his side.

"Hello. How do you feel?"

"I'm not sure. My head hurts terribly, and my body is stiff."

"I will fix you a tea from your herbs," she told him as she laid the squirrels down to fix the tea.

His questioning dark-sapphire eyes followed every move she made.

"I found you on the ground and have been taking care of you. What is your name?"

When he didn't answer, she looked up, surprised at the expression on his face.

"What is it? Are you in more pain?"

"No...I don't know who I am," came the whisper from his lips.

"What? You can't remember who you are! Why are you here?"

"I don't know."

"Here, drink this, and perhaps you will feel better and remember," she said as she helped him sit up.

Dizziness overwhelmed him, and he leaned into her shoulder.

"What is your name?" he whispered.

"I am Emily Rose Adams from Texas."

He turned to stare up at her as if something clicked but would not come forward before he drank from the offered cup.

She laid him back down, moving away as quickly as possible.

She stared back for a few moments before turning because she felt a great sadness. She had injured him, and it might have caused his memory loss. Well, at least she didn't carry the guilt of killing him.

Later, after cooking the squirrel meat and mixing it into thick gravy, she helped him sit up again, handing him a plate of squirrel gravy and campfire biscuits.

He complained of dizziness again, but it soon lessened, and he was able to feed himself.

"You are a great cook. Thanks." Feeling better, he eased himself back down, pulling the blanket over his shoulders.

He slept.

Emily Rose was thankful he was healing, and he had eaten for the first time in days. But who was he, and what was she to do with him?

For the first time, she let herself really look at him. His features were handsome, invoking a rush to her senses. His skin was brown—perhaps tanned from the sun—and she knew his eyes were blue. Strange he would choose to dress as an Indian, but in reality, he was a white man. Maybe he was a half-breed...That would account for his confusion.

Was he confused? He was now, since she had shot him. Finding no answers to her questions, she cleaned up from supper, put large pieces of wood on the fire, and went to sleep.

The early mornings were cool in the mountains, and Emily Rose was up early to put more wood on the fire and start coffee. She sat wrapped in her blanket as she enjoyed his supply of coffee. Looking at his sleeping form, she saw that he had not yet stirred.

"Good morning," he said as he woke. "I feel like a cup of coffee, if you don't mind waiting on me. I am still very dizzy." He pushed up slowly to lean back against a large tree.

After pouring him coffee, she took it over to him, saying, "You look like an Indian, but you speak perfect English. How come?"

"My father was a Ute medicine man, and my mother was white. I have had the pleasure of living in both their worlds."

"What is your name, and where do you come from?"

Blinking several times, Black Hawk replied, "I don't know."

"You just told me about your parents, but you don't know who you are. Strange. It must be the head injury."

"Do you know what happened to me? I have flashes of memory, but nothing is connected or makes sense."

Emily Rose was silent for a while before replying, "I believe someone shot you. When I found you, you were lying on the ground, bleeding."

"Oh. What were you doing out here alone?"

"I...uh...escaped from a band of Apaches who had kidnapped me down in Texas."

"You're from Texas? Something about Texas rings in my mind, but I can't remember what it is."

"Do you think you are from Texas? Maybe that's why. What would you like me to call you until you remember what your name is?"

Black Hawk thought for a moment before saying, "Call me Levi. That sounds like a name I would like."

"OK, Levi it is, until you get back your memories. How about breakfast? I found several turkey eggs yesterday when I was hunting."

After they had eaten, he went back to sleep after drinking more of the herbal tea. She took the pans to the stream and washed them as she planned how to get home. What should she do about the stranger? When he was better, should she leave him here or take him with her?

When she returned to camp, she grabbed her rifle, heading out to do more hunting. Spotting several deer and elk, she passed them by, knowing they were too large for her to handle and the meat would ruin before they could eat it all. She looked for smaller game.

When she returned to camp later in the afternoon, Levi was sitting up, leaning against the tree, watching for her return.

"Thought for a while you might have left me but saw your horse grazing with Powder and was relieved you were coming back."

"You remembered your horse's name. What's yours?"

Again the look of confusion on his face as he said, "I don't know."

"Oh well, things are beginning to come back; it will, too. I shot two small turkeys, which will keep us in meat until tomorrow. Do you feel like helping me remove the feathers?"

"Sure."

Hours later they were pleased to be full of roasted turkey and coffee as they settled down for the night.

"Where in Texas are you from?"

"My parents have a cattle ranch near San Antonio."

"San Antonio. For some reason, I have a connection there."

"We have been here for a number of days since your accident, and I need to start trying to get home. But I don't know what to do with you. Would you like to go with me? Do you think you could ride if we broke camp tomorrow morning?"

"I am feeling better than I did. If I start to feel bad, we can always stop early."

"I don't know where we are. What I have in mind is to ride east until we find someone who can give us directions. There are army forts around, but I don't know if we are close to any of them."

After a quick breakfast the next morning, they packed up and headed down the mountain. After bouncing for several hours, Levi had to stop and rest before they continued. His head was hurting, and he was feeling sick to his stomach.

Emily Rose helped settle him in a comfortable spot and built a small fire to heat water in the coffeepot. After it boiled, she mixed some of his herbs in a cup, allowing them to steep before giving the tea to him.

Levi drank the herbal tea and soon went to sleep. Not wanting to stop so soon, Emily Rose paced for a while, trying to decide what to do. Grabbing her rifle, she left to hunt for supper. She hoped he would feel like traveling again before it got dark.

An hour later when she returned, he was sitting up and feeling better. They decided to continue until dark if he could make it.

They managed to travel until late evening, making camp near a small flowing river. Levi moved around the camp, picking up wood for the fire. Emily Rose placed small rocks around a hole she had dug in the sand for the fire. Putting small kindling in the hole, she soon had a fire kicking to life from the flint rock Levi had in his saddlebags.

Cleaning the two squirrels she had shot earlier, she placed them over the fire after she had skewered them on green sticks.

Levi sat down quickly, saying, "I'm sorry I don't have the strength to hobble the horses."

"I can do it. I am glad you were able to get this far. Please rest now. The meat will be ready soon."

When she returned, he was asleep. She hated to wake him, but he needed food as well as rest to grow stronger. After shaking him awake, she handed him one of the roasted squirrels and a cup of coffee, saying, "Hope you like the seasoning I put on it." She laughed.

Levi looked questioningly at her, but she just shrugged and said, "I'll tell you the story sometime."

As soon as Levi had finished eating, he lay down, falling asleep the minute he stretched out. Emily Rose settled down by the fire after she had cleaned up from supper. She poured herself a cup of coffee and looked at the strange man across from her. She was full of questions and no answers. *Will his memories return? Did he see who shot him? What should I do with him? I feel responsible for him. Where is his family? How can I contact them?*

Finding no solutions, she wrapped her blanket around her and prayed she could find someone to help them very soon.

18

The Twins

The ride back to San Antonio from the border was fast and silent. They arrived hungry and angry...well, Captain Jones was angry with all of them because they didn't complete their mission. He was furious with them because they were turned back by a vision. A vision!

Will and Eli had very little to say on the trip back. Arriving in San Antonio late in the evening, they decided to stay in their rooms at the Menger Hotel before reporting to their families that they did not find Emily Rose.

After ordering steak dinners to be brought to their rooms, both men hurried upstairs for hot baths to wash the trail dust off.

Later, as they finished their meal, Will commented to Eli, "You haven't said much about the vision. What do you think it truly meant?"

"It frightened me at first, but I have had days now to think about it. It was sent to warn us to return to San Antonio. The reason is not clear yet. It was a warning for Captain Jones to stay away from that place on the border. That in itself should have been enough. I know he was sullen about returning, but it could have been very dangerous for all of us if we had not heeded the warning."

"You're right about that. But there was so much more I couldn't talk about. Seeing Silver really shook me, especially knowing that Black Hawk had been shot. I saw it so vividly, as if it was me getting killed."

"We don't know if he is dead. He may only be injured. I want to believe that seeing Silver near camp was a sign Black Hawk is still alive. Was there anything in your dream about Emily Rose?"

A long silence filled the room before Eli sighed, saying, "I don't know what she looks like, but it was as if I knew she was nearby in the area...like I sensed her presence. But how can that be?" Shudders shook his body as he searched his memories, trying to figure out what it meant.

"Have you had any more visions? Or knowings, as Sadie and Marty call them?"

"No, nothing since that morning."

"Well, let's get some sleep. I am looking forward to sleeping in a real bed again. Those nights on the trail in a bedroll were hard on my back."

"Yes, they were. Good night, Will. Sleep well."

Early the next morning, after a hearty breakfast, the brothers rode out to Rowdy's to give him a firsthand report of what happened.

As they rode up, the guard dogs began to bark, but Will quieted them with a silent thought and a slight hand movement.

"I wish I could do that instead of having visions," Eli whispered to Will as they got down from their horses.

Rowdy came out on the porch, surprised, with a worried look on his face at seeing both back so soon. "Howdy, boys. Come on in for some coffee."

Once they had looped the reins over the fence posts and wiped their feet at the front door as their mother had taught them, they followed Rowdy into the kitchen.

Worry was in Rowdy's voice as he called Ruth to come back in the house from feeding the chickens. His children had seen the men ride in and hurried into the kitchen with their mother. Rowdy motioned for

Will and Eli to sit down at the table as he poured hot coffee into their cups.

Ruth stopped with a gasp when she saw the brothers at her table and no Emily Rose. "Oh my God, has something happened to her?"

"I don't know, Ruth. They just got here."

"We did not mean to frighten either of you. We don't know anything about her. We turned back a few days ago because of an incident that happened to Eli. I'll let him tell you about it."

All eyes turned to Eli as he stuttered. "I...uh...was asleep and had a dream or a vision about our brother, Black Hawk, being shot. It was so clear, as if I was the one who was shot..."

"Was he killed?"

"I don't know. I saw it happen, and I jerked awake, screaming. When I opened my eyes, Silver was sitting at the edge of our camp. Silver was Mother's wolf that was always with her. I was so afraid I did not know what to do, but I also was given a warning for Captain Jones not to go to Tres Jacales. Death waited for him there. He was livid when I told him in front of the other Rangers, and they refused to continue. So we all returned last night."

"And Emily Rose?" whispered her mother.

"There was nothing about her but a feeling that she is all right. That is all."

"Your mother had special powers and an aura around her. I remember her wolf. He always stayed near her when she was working alone. He was her protector, she said. But how can he still be alive after all this time? That was more than twenty years ago, and he's here now?"

Will spoke then. "I saw him at her cabin just before we left to come here. Then Eli said he was at our campsite here in Texas, and it shook me up. I have no explanation for that. Do you?"

"Unless he is watching over us as he did Mother," whispered Eli.

"We need to visit with Jim but wanted you to know first why we are back." Will stood up quickly to end the conversation before it got into things he knew nothing about.

Hannah, who had been silent as she listened to the brothers, now asked her parents, "May I ride over to see Susan?"

"If it is all right with the boys, you may go."

"Sure, we welcome your company," Will replied with a big grin on his attractive face.

"I'll get my horse and meet you out front," she yelled over her shoulder as she dashed out, dressed in her tight work pants.

Her parents looked at each other, surprised at how Hannah was so giddy.

Later, a pleased Hannah rode between the two gorgeous brothers. "Am I related to both of you?"

Embarrassed by her bluntness, Eli said, "Well, since you and I have the same father, I guess that makes us half brother and sister."

Turning toward Will, she asked, "Does that make us kin, since Eli is your brother?"

Will stuttered before he answered, "Eli and I have the same mother but different fathers. So since you are not related to my mother and my father, I think not."

"But how come you two are twins if you have two different fathers? How could that be?"

A fit of coughing erupted from both brothers, causing their horses to dance around in the road.

"Uh, Hannah, talk to your mother about that. It is too delicate for us to discuss with you," stammered a red-faced Eli.

"But I know about the birds and the bees. Is that why you two are acting so embarrassed? I know what men and women—"

Both men spurred their horses into a gallop before any more conversation could be heard and left Hannah in the dust.

Hannah spurred her stallion into a gallop as she chased after the brothers.

Racing up to the ranch house, they found Jim sitting on the front porch. Surprised to see Will, Eli, and Hannah, he stood up sluggishly, using his cane to reach the railing for support.

"Hello! Come on in."

The riders swung down from their horses, leaving the reins looped to the hitching post as Hannah preceded them to the porch. Will's eyes watched Hannah's cute little butt bounce up the front steps.

Eli gave him a dirty look.

Giving Jim a big hug, Hannah said, "It is wonderful to see you up and doing so much better, Uncle Jim. Is Susan here?"

"Yes, she is in the kitchen with Mary Lee. Go on in."

Jim shook Eli's hand, then gave Will a big hug. "Boy, I'm proud to see you. Surprised you are back early."

Receiving only nods from the men, he motioned for them to go into the house and followed them into the living room as he yelled at Mary Lee, "Bring us some coffee!"

When they had been served and everyone had gathered around to hear the young men's story, Will and then Eli related the tale to Jim and his family.

Amazement showed on their faces as they stared at first one man, then the other. First to recover his voice, Jim asked, "Have you ever had a vision before, Eli?"

"No, sir, I haven't. It was so real I could see the bullet coming at me but in slow motion. I even felt it as it hit my...uh...Black Hawk's head. He went flying backward, and I saw Powder, his horse. That's how I knew it was him. I was yelling when I woke up. I know I frightened the camp, too. Did you know about Mother's wolf, Silver?"

Shocked at first about the question, Jim was slow to respond, "I saw him many times at the edge of the forest or lingering close to her if she was alone. She always said they talked to each other. But I never saw it."

"The night we were born, Tuffy Sawyer from the trading post tried to kill Mother and hurt us. Marty Long, a friend of Mother's, protected her and ran Tuffy outside. Silver tracked him down and killed him. We never knew anything about the incident until we read her journals. Did you know who Tuffy was?"

"Yes, she was fearful of him. He was a very bad man and tried many times to cheat or harm her. Glad to know he was taken care of."

Mary Lee could see the brothers were distressed and quickly assigned chores for the younger children as she hurried them out of the room. But Susan and Hannah hung back to be near them.

With nothing more to say, Will and Eli stood up, planning to leave, but Susan asked Jim, "Could we show Will and Eli around the ranch before lunch? We won't be long."

"That would be fine, if they are not in a hurry."

"We would be honored to have two beautiful ladies show us the ranch," replied Will as he looked at Hannah her cheeks blushed almost the color of her hair.

Jim nodded his consent as Susan ran for her bonnet. They soon left the house and walked toward the horse barn.

The brothers smiled at each other, as they knew interesting things could happen in a barn.

19

Emily Rose

Emily Rose and her "mystery man" had been traveling for days following the wide, meandering river as it grew from a small stream to a river. She could tell the stress of the trip was telling on Levi, but he did not complain. She laughed to herself, thinking about the "stoic Indian suffering in silence," but not in a mean way. She was glad he didn't complain. God knew she wanted to.

There were advantages to following the river. One was the availability of water. Emily Rose was quick to remember the hot days when she'd gone without it. And her biggest hope was it would lead to a town so she could find out where she was and get help notifying her family she was alive. She enjoyed wearing Levi's clothes, but after long, hot days on the trail, she needed to bathe. She switched out her outfits whenever they began to smell. Then she washed her raggedy dress and underthings and let them dry while she bathed in the river.

If her clothes did not completely dry, she would place them on sticks near the fire. Levi usually fell asleep as soon as he had eaten and did not awaken until morning. He seemed to be a gentle soul, even though he was an Indian or at least half-Indian. At least he was not like the others, who had mistreated her as if she were not human.

She did most of the work in camp and all the hunting. He had told her he was seeing double and it was impossible for him to hunt with a rifle. He could set snares if necessary. But it wasn't. She was a good shot.

Seven long days and nights on the trail were finally coming to an end. When they set up camp the last night, they had seen lights in the distance of a town down in the river valley. As they ate supper, which was only roasted meat and water now, since they had run out of their meager supplies days earlier, they made plans to break camp at sunrise to get to the town before evening.

Early the next morning, they were up and moving, trying to get across the open valley before the sun got too hot. Emily Rose guessed the date to be late May or early June, but she couldn't be sure. She had been taken at Easter in April and had lost track of days and weeks since.

Weariness had set in by the time they reached the main street in late afternoon and she searched for the name of the town.

"Pecos, Texas! Hurray! I'm back in Texas at last."

Stopping at the Orient Hotel, she hoped to get rooms for them but remembered she did not have any money. Looking at Levi, she said, "Do you have any money?"

"Money?" he asked with a blank stare.

"Oh, I guess you don't need money where you live. We need money here to get rooms for us. Well, let's go in and see what we need to do to get rooms."

Sliding down from her horse, she waited for him to do the same, as she noticed they were drawing a crowd.

She realized how they must look with her in her ragged Easter dress and filthy bonnet and Levi dressed in buckskins with the comical head dressing she had done. She grabbed his arm as she led the way into the lobby.

Walking up to the desk clerk, who looked down his nose in disdain, she announced in her most upper-class voice, "I would like two rooms for my injured friend and myself, please."

Without hesitation the clerk spewed out, "We don't allow his kind in this hotel. Get out!"

Shocked at the hatred and the viciousness in his whiny voice, she drew back. "What do you mean, his kind?"

"He's an Indian! And he does not stay in this hotel! And since you are an Injun lover, neither will you."

Hearing laughter from behind her, Emily Rose turned to see people watching from the doorway to see what happened next.

"My friend is injured and needs care. We need a place to rest. Won't anyone here help us?" she pleaded.

No one answered.

The crowd backed onto the boardwalk as they moved away from them. No one would help.

Emily Rose took Levi by the arm, leading him proudly outside. She glanced up and down the street, looking for another hotel. Laughter and finger pointing followed them as she took the reins of their horses and led them away from the jeering group.

Levi remained silent.

Leaving Main Street, they crossed over to Church Street. Noticing a sign at the end of the dusty lane announcing "Mrs. Byington's Boardinghouse," Emily Rose stopped to stare at the freshly painted white house with an attractive older woman sweeping the front steps.

"Excuse me. Are you Mrs. Byington?"

"Yes, I am. May I help you?" she said as she walked toward the odd-looking couple.

"I'm Emily Rose Adams. We need a place to stay until my injured friend can recover. Do you have any rooms?"

Mrs. Byington looked at the dusty, travel-weary pair before answering. "Young lady, you are traveling in the company of an Indian. And you want me to allow you to stay in my home?"

"If you hear our story, perhaps you will change your mind about us. On Easter Sunday near San Antonio, a gang of outlaws attacked my family, and I was kidnapped. They killed my father and several others. This was my new Easter dress. I have lived in it since. A week or so after that, I was traded to Apaches, who took me somewhere into New Mexico. I managed to escape them and stumbled across this poor man who had been shot. For days I wasn't sure if he would live or die, but as you can see, he is barely well enough to travel. We have been on the road for about seven days now, are out of food and totally exhausted. Can you find it in your heart to help us?" pleaded Emily Rose.

Taken aback by her story, Mrs. Byington took her arm, leading her toward her home as she said, "You poor dear. How awful for you. Yes, yes, I will help you."

"And my friend also?" she said as she stopped to look back at Levi, who followed in silence.

"What is your friend's name?"

"I don't know. He has lost his memory. I am calling him Levi."

"Does he speak English?"

"Mrs. Byington, I am fluent in several languages, and English happens to be one of them. Since I was shot, I can't remember my name or where I belong. I thank you for your generous offer to help us. We have no money now, but you will be generously repaid at a later date."

Both women stared wide-eyed and openmouthed at Levi after his eloquent speech.

And his intense dark-blue eyes stared back.

Emily Rose was the first to regain her voice by saying, "You are full of surprises, aren't you, Levi?"

Mrs. Byington noticed his dark-blue eyes for the first time, thinking he was white or a half-breed at the least.

"Very well, come along, and I will show you to your rooms. This is a respectable boardinghouse I run here. There are certain rules. One of which is the ladies sleep upstairs, and the gentlemen sleep downstairs. Here is your room, first door on the right, Levi. After we get some food in you, I will show you to your room, Emily Rose. I think I have some dresses my daughter left that may fit you. Levi, I will have to send out for clothes for you. And baths certainly are in order as well. But first things first. You both look like you are starving, and I won't have that in my house."

While they were eating, Mrs. Byington sent one of her other boarders to get the doctor. When the doctor arrived, he was reluctant to treat an Indian, but when Mrs. Byington threatened him with not allowing him to eat at her table again, he relented.

Dr. Springer was an old country doctor who had seen better days. He had traveled for years in and out of Pecos, delivering babies, patching up bullet holes, and sewing up people, including gory amputations from all types of accidents. But he had never seen anyone healed by the herbs the woman had been using on the Indian.

"It's amazing how well both head injuries have healed, considering all you had was Indian remedies to work with. You have what is known as amnesia. It occurs when you have a severe brain injury. In your case, you had two head traumas—the gunshot wound and then hitting the back of your head when you fell off your horse. Will your memories return? I don't know. But it is encouraging that you are beginning to remember things. The line of the bullet cut through your hair and scalp, burning quite a streak. A little more this way and you would be dead, and we would not be having this conversation. I will put this salve on the burn and wrap it back up. You might consider cutting your hair so the wound will get more air."

Levi shook his head.

"Well, you will still have a long scar in your dark hair until the hair above can grow over it. It's your choice."

Levi just grunted.

— —

After the doctor left, Levi went to his room to lie down and wait his turn to bathe. He had so much to think about. The most life-shattering experience he had ever had was the rejection at the hotel because he was Indian and a half-breed.

He had never been treated like that before—or at least he had never been rejected because he was an Indian. His white family and Indian family were kind and loving, but that had always been his world, which never included anyone from outside. His mother had made sure of that. Now he was beginning to understand why—and to remember as well.

He tried to force himself to remember more, but all he saw was darkness when he tried to force his thoughts out. His memories came when he did not expect them, as if they slipped out. Sadness filled his heart as he drifted off to sleep.

He dreamed of happier times with Mother and Father. He dreamed of his Indian family. He dreamed of the snow-white mountains with the black river and the red rose dripping blood.

He saw the bullet coming toward him, fired from a rifle like Emily Rose's rifle. He jerked awake, covered in cold sweat.

He was remembering!

He leaped from the bed and paced the room. He must not forget what he dreamed. He must remember everything. He clung to his dream, hanging on to the very essence of himself.

20

Emily Rose

Emily Rose was up early the next morning, heading toward the sheriff's office. During the night, the thought of what she must do to get home had come to her: find a Ranger! The sheriff seemed like the most likely person to start with to accomplish that.

After knocking loudly on the office door, she heard a muffled "Come in."

"Sheriff, I need to talk with you," she said as she pushed the heavy door open.

"I'm surprised anyone would knock. Most times they just bust right in. Come in, young lady," he said as he jumped to his feet and offered her a chair. "How may I help you?"

"Well, sheriff, I am looking for a Texas Ranger. Are any of them around here?"

"Uh...can I help you? I am the sheriff."

"Yes, sir, I know. But I need to contact one of them. Are any of them here or not?"

"What is your name?"

"I'm sorry. I didn't mean to be rude. I should have introduced my-self. My name is Emily Rose Adams from San Antonio. My father is a Texas Ranger, and I need to find a Ranger."

"Well, I am expecting Ranger Bailey here any day. He is stationed out of El Paso but comes through here often. It's about time for him."

"Ranger George Bailey? That's wonderful. I know him, and he can help me. When he gets here, please ask him to come to Mrs. Byington's boardinghouse. Thank you so much, sheriff."

Excited that Ranger Bailey was coming, Emily Rose rushed back to the boardinghouse in time to help Mrs. Byington clean up the breakfast dishes. She related her news to her and Levi. "The Ranger who is ex-pected knows my father and can help me get back home."

Levi looked surprised she was leaving so soon.

She noticed his anxiety and was quick to respond with, "But of course, you will be coming with me. I can't leave you behind until we find out who you are. You are quite a mystery."

Later in the afternoon, Mrs. Byington knocked on Emily Rose's door upstairs to let her know she had a visitor in the parlor. Anxious to see who it was, she followed Mrs. Byington down the stairs to the parlor.

"Oh, Georgie, you came," she squealed as she leaped into the rang-er's outstretched arms. He swung her around.

"Em, you are alive. Bless your soul. Are you all right?"

Turning to catch her breath from the excitement, she replied, "I am glad you are here. It has been terrible, but I am now safe, thanks to Mrs. Byington and the others who have helped us. Georgie, will you help me get home please?" Tears of joy and sadness streamed down her face.

"Now, now, Em, don't cry. First thing we need to do is go to the telegraph office and wire Captain Jones you are safe and let your parents know you are alive."

"My father is alive...but I saw him and Jim killed."

"The good news is Jim was shot in the leg and is pretty crippled up. Your father was shot in the head, and it was touch-and-go for a while, but he is better. The bad news is that Rachael, Jim's wife, was killed.

Then you got kidnapped. When Blackjack killed the gang, and you were not with them, we were so worried."

"Oh no. I remember Aunt Rachael falling from the wagon. I'm so sorry," she said, covering her face to hide her tears of sorrow.

"How did you escape being killed when the outlaws were attacked?"

Mrs. Byington handed Emily Rose a handkerchief to wipe her tears. Looking up at George, Emily Rose replied to his question. "I was traded to a band of Apaches before that happened, I guess. They took me somewhere into the New Mexico mountains. When I escaped one night, I stole the leader's stallion and rode away. Several days later, I found Levi injured."

"That's quite a story, Emily Rose. Try to put it behind you. You are safe now. But there will be much joy when we let your family know you have been found safe. Now we need to figure out what train to put you on to get back to San Antonio."

"Trains, of course. I never thought about them. I thought you would have to take us back across country. I was dreading another trek across hot, dry Texas."

"Us? Who is us?"

"My...uh...friend, Levi. I met him along the way and promised to help him get home, too," she stammered.

"Where is this friend?"

"I found him shot in the head up in the mountains and have brought him here."

At that moment, Levi, who had been listening from his bedroom, stepped out into the hallway and walked toward the Ranger. He was dressed in his buckskins and moccasins, his knife at his waist. A white turban, courtesy of the doctor, adorned his head, which gave him a comical look.

Ranger Bailey's gun hand inched toward his weapon. Emily Rose saw the slight movement and berated him. "Shame on you, Georgie. My friend Levi is in need of our help. He has been shot in the head and can't remember who he is."

"But he's still an Injun, and I don't trust Injuns."

"Well, you will have to get over that notion for now. This is Levi. That's what we are calling him for now until he can remember who he is. Levi, come over and shake hands with Ranger Bailey."

Both men glared at each other before Emily Rose grabbed an arm on each and pulled them close enough to shake hands.

Levi spoke first between clenched teeth. "Pleased to meet ya, Ranger. Glad you will be able to help Emily Rose get home."

Ranger Bailey gave a few grunts before dropping his hand. It was obvious from his body language he hated Indians and did not like touching this one.

"When can we go to the telegraph office? I have never sent a telegram, and I want to know how to do it. Will you be coming with us? Oh, I hope so. I don't know anything about riding on a train. How long will it take us to get back home?"

"Gracious, Emily Rose. Will you slow down talking? You are wearing me out. Yes, we will go now if you are ready."

"Let me get my bonnet, and I'll be ready. Want to go with us, Levi?"

"No, thanks."

After they left, Levi turned to Mrs. Byington and asked, "Do you know how to cut hair?"

It was late in the day before Ranger Bailey escorted Emily Rose back to the boardinghouse. He visited with Mrs. Byington and left tickets and instructions on the time and train she was to put them on tomorrow morning. He had pressing Ranger business and could not stay. Taking his leave of her had been difficult for him.

Emily Rose was tearful as he told her goodbye. He got a little misty-eyed, too, because he was pleased this story would have a happy ending. His friend Rowdy would be happy the Easter nightmare would finally be over.

21

Levi

Who is the man in the mirror?

Levi considered the man's features as he turned his head this way and that. The emotions playing out in the glass were amazing.

Confusion. Yes, he was certainly confused about who shot him and who he was. Fear. The fear of the unknown was enough to drive anyone crazy. And being taken along with Emily Rose to God only knew where was unnerving. Was he losing himself? But who was he?

Was he nice-looking for a white man? Were the blue eyes an asset or a curse? What about the dent in the middle of his chin? Was it appealing to a woman?

He ran his fingers through the now short black hair, which had curled slightly since the weight of the long braids was gone. *My braids?* He picked up both braids, looking at the proof he had really cut them off. Was he abandoning his Indian ways? But what were his Indian ways?

He touched the widow's peak of his hairline and remembered his mother calling it that. When he tried to remember her, there was only blankness. But at times, like now, something would slip through. He outlined his dark eyebrows and looked at his prominent nose. His skin was dark brown from living his entire life outdoors in the mountains. Again, another thought had slipped through.

He had removed his shirt to shake off the cut hair and now stared at the male body in the mirror. He had never looked at himself before. Tanned skin covered a muscular body. His arms were solid and strong as he flexed, causing the muscles to tighten. He had no extra weight around his middle to show he had led an easy life.

Would Emily Rose like this body?

Don't torture yourself with questions like that, he chided himself. *She is a white woman who is used to white ways—not Indian ways.* His body ignored his will to remain passive; when he thought of the beautiful Emily Rose, his breathing increased as his body longed to touch her.

From the moment he began to revive after his "accident," his eyes had followed her. His first thoughts of her had been of a raggedy angel who had come down to care for a dying man. But when she spoke, her sweet voice made his soul rejoice. He watched her when she did not know he was watching.

He had pretended sleep when she bathed in the river and slept naked as she waited for her clothes to dry. He had caught glimpses of her shapely body when her blanket fell open as she worked around the campfire to place her clothes on rocks and sticks to dry. And early mornings, a shapely leg would be exposed as she slept.

He had begun to learn what desire for a woman felt like. He had never felt this way before. The women he knew in his village did not appeal to him. Was it his punishment to desire a white woman he could never have?

Since they had gotten to Pecos, she had blossomed like a red rosebud opening its petals to display its beauty.

A tingling in his head came from an old memory that would not emerge about a red rose. What did it mean? And now he would do anything she wanted him to do—even look like a white man!

The mirror he was so intently gazing into hung on the wall near the door of his room. He was still staring into the mirror when Emily Rose burst into his room with a quick knock.

She shrieked! She was startled he was so close and surprised to see him half-naked.

"I'm so sorry! I should not have burst into your room without your invitation," she said as she turned aside but not before she got a picture of suntanned skin stretched over a gorgeous, muscular back when he whirled to grab his shirt.

"I was trying to get accustomed to not having braids. I don't look like me."

"You cut your hair! You are beautiful...I mean, handsome. I can't believe what a difference it makes. I'm glad you have removed the bandage. Without it, I am not constantly reminded of your head wound."

"And that bothers you?"

"Yes, I mean, of course. The thought someone would shoot a handsome and virile man like you—I mean, it musta been someone who didn't know who you were," she stammered.

"You think I am handsome and virile just because I am dressed as a white man and cut my hair now. I am the same man I was with my Indian clothes and my braids. I still have no memories."

"Oh yes, you are. I didn't mean to sound as if I was criticizing your previous life. How could I when I don't know what kind of life you led? But we can find out together."

"Hmm...I like that idea very much," he said, moving toward Emily Rose. He backed her into the corner behind the door. Somewhere along the way, his shirt dropped to the floor.

Her hands came up to rest on his brawny chest as she felt the heat emanating from him as his body crowded her closer to the wall, but he kept just enough distance so they were not touching. It was tantalizing. She waited expectantly as she stretched her arms around his neck, drawing him closer to her warming embrace.

He rested his hands on her slim hips, fighting the urges to roam over her luscious body.

Levi's dark-blue eyes gazed into her innocent green ones. "Do you know what I want to do with you?"

Auburn curls wiggled back and forth as she nodded, then shook her head no.

"I have wanted to taste your lips from the moment I opened my eyes and you were standing over me."

A breathless whisper slid over her lips. "You have?"

"Would you like for me to show you now?"

Again the auburn curls wiggled back and forth with consent.

Levi leaned toward her as he stared at her rosy red lips. He longed to feel them under his. He smiled as he placed a tiny kiss on her upturned nose. His heart stopped as she whispered, "Yes, oh yes."

When their lips touched, a magical spell swirled around them, surrounding and concealing the couple as if they were in a secret cocoon hidden behind the door, invisible to the outside world.

Levi pressed her willing body back against the wall as he led the way into unknown emotions. As inexperienced as she, he allowed his soul to guide him to the next step.

He liked the feel of his hard arousal pressing into the juncture of her legs. He felt the heat of their bodies rubbing and moving against each other. And he wanted more.

Emily Rose was lost in a whirlwind going on inside her body. She was drawn to this being in her arms. She loved the feel of his body pressing into hers. The desire was rising. She wanted him! She wanted all of him! Right now!

"Emily Rose! Are you here?" Mrs. Byington called from the hallway, jarring the flaming hot couple from their tryst behind the bedroom door.

"Oh my, Levi. That was wonderful. Maybe later, uh, we can talk again. I have to go now; Mrs. Byington is calling me," she whispered in his ear as she glided sadly away from his blazing hot body. Hurrying to quiet a loud Mrs. Byington, she moved down the hallway toward the kitchen.

"Mrs. Byington, I am here. Did you need something?"

"Yes, dear, would you peel the potatoes for dinner?" She had seen the couple embracing between the crack in the door and knew she had to stop it before it got out of hand. *Yes, young love has hung heavy in this house since their arrival*, she thought as she wiped her hands and went back to making a pie for the residents.

Levi closed his bedroom door, disappointed they had been interrupted. He wanted more of Emily Rose. But a new feeling was swimming to the top of his world. Was this what was called lust? Or was it a true feeling he had for Emily Rose? He thought the latter was true. The excitement between them had developed over the time they had been together, and it grew with each passing moment.

Levi walked back to the mirror. This time, he had a different attitude toward the man in the reflecting glass.

22

The Twins

The telegram caused quite a ruckus when it arrived at Captain Frank Jones's office in San Antonio. As a rule, telegrams were bad news, so when the dispatcher brought it in and commented it was about Emily Rose, Captain Frank was reluctant to open it.

He opened the telegram with shaking hands, afraid of how the news contained within would forever change his friends' lives. After scanning it, he shouted with joy, causing the other Rangers to jump for their guns.

"Emily Rose Adams has been found safe and sound. She will be arriving next week on a train. Joe, will you saddle my horse? I'm heading to Rowdy's with the good news."

He rode as fast as he could to bring them the happy news.

When he arrived, he was all smiles as he told Rowdy to round up the family because he had good news about Emily Rose. When they were assembled, including Eli, he read the following to them:

Emily Rose safe in Pecos with me. Stop. Em leaving tomorrow on Texas Pacific 49 to Fort Worth. Stop. Change trains to San Antonio and home. Stop. Arriving in seven days. Stop. Ranger George Bailey

Ruth and Hannah were crying and hugging each other. A tearful Rowdy, overcome with joy and relief, sat down as his sons gathered around him and wiped tears of happiness from their eyes.

Eli shook Captain Jones's hand, saying, "Thank you for bringing us this amazing news. I know Rowdy and Ruth have fought despair for a long time. Also, I hope you are not still angry at me for the unsuccessful trip."

"I must say I was not prepared for what happened. But Emily Rose was found in Pecos, and that's a long way from where we were headed. I am anxious to visit with her and find out all that has happened."

"Captain Jones, please remember the warning you were given regarding going to Tres Jacales. It's for your own protection."

"Thanks, Eli, I'll keep that in mind. Rowdy, I am heading back to town. Glad I could deliver such wonderful news."

Rowdy jumped up to shake his friend's hand and slap him on the back as he walked with him to his horse. Eli followed close behind as he told them his plans.

"I'm riding over to Jim's to see Will and give them the wonderful news. Bye for now."

Eli had time to think about the past month's events as he rode over to Jim's ranch. He had been surprised to discover he and Will had separate fathers, and coming to Texas to meet both had been emotionally taxing as well. And now Emily Rose was coming home: his half sister. How would she react when she learned she had an older brother she knew nothing about? Probably like he would if someone new appeared in his family line.

The ranch dogs heard him riding up and set up a big commotion before Will quieted them down with a nod.

Eli laughed. "Up to your old tricks again, I see."

"Hey, little brother, good to see you today. What brings you over? I sense there is something we need to know."

"Strange you would say it like that. Are you truly having inklings of things to come?"

"That phrasing popped out. I was not expecting to say anything like that. But I seem to know the news is about Emily Rose, and she is safe."

Eli stared transfixed at his brother. Had he guessed it, or had it come to him?

"Well, you tell me, big brother. What do you know about Emily Rose?"

Will opened his mouth several times, but nothing came out. Staring hard at Eli, he said, "Emily Rose has been found safe and is heading home. Train. On a train."

"How do you know that? Did Captain Jones come here before heading back to town?"

"I am at as much of a loss as you, Eli. It popped into my head as soon as I saw you ride up. Is that what you are coming to tell us?"

"Call the family together, Will, and I will make the announcement before you scare them all with your newfound ability."

Following Will into the house, Eli wondered again for the umpteenth time today what was happening to his family. *Are we all going crazy? What next?* Would their sister, Raven, fly in on the wings of a raven? Or Black Hawk...He left it at that, since he did not know Black Hawk's condition or whereabouts.

It was almost lunchtime when he arrived, and after Will rang the dinner bell and everyone gathered around the table, Eli made the announcement that Emily Rose would be arriving next week on the train.

The meal progressed in a jovial mood after that until Jim became melancholy as he remarked, "I only wish Rachael was coming on the train with her."

The table went silent.

Jim rose and limped out to the family cemetery with his shoulders slumped. No one spoke for a few minutes before Mary Lee stood up and wanted to know who wanted pie.

The conversation resumed.

"Will, I would like to talk with you outside. Let's walk down to the river."

Will followed Eli outside, wondering if he wanted to talk about Will's strangeness. Of course, Eli was having visions, and they both were getting weird.

When they were far enough away not to be overheard, Eli asked, "I am thinking we should take the train and meet Emily Rose in Fort Worth. She might get on the wrong train if someone is not there to meet her. What do you think?"

"That sounds good, but how will we do it?"

"That I don't know yet, but let's ride into town and see what we can figure out. Just don't say anything to the others about what we are thinking."

"I'll go saddle up. Get your horse and meet me at the barn. We'll leave from there."

23

The Twins

"Well, that was is an interesting outcome. We came to town to buy tickets on the train, and now we own the train."

"Quite amazing. Actually, little brother, we now own a railroad. It is our first investment with the money Mother left us. Now we have control over when and where it will go."

"Gentlemen, are you ready to take a look at what you have purchased?" asked Mr. Elgin, who had brokered the train transaction.

"Yes, let's go look at what we bought. Where is it parked? And how long has it been sitting?"

"It's parked on a side track near the turnabout wheel. The previous owner passed away several weeks ago, and his will instructed the railroad business be sold."

They were deep in thought about what they had purchased and hopeful it was not a bad investment, since they had become overexcited and bought it sight unseen. But it seemed the right thing to do in the moment. Praying the impulse was a good one, they crossed over numerous tracks in the rail yard, passing several cold engines before they saw their newly acquired train.

The Pecos Express sat on the last track in the yard. It was obvious it had not been moved in weeks; a layer of wood cinders spewed by passing trains covered the engine and the cars. Number 1313 was painted on the side of the engine. "Pecos Express Railroad" was splashed across the coal car in bright-yellow letters. It had two cattle cars, one passenger car, a dining car, and a red caboose, and the last was a VIP car.

As the brothers looked at each other, Will remarked, "I hope the number on the engine is a sign of a good investment instead of a sucker deal of bad luck."

"With all the weird stuff happening to us lately, I am going to look at it as a good omen. It will be what we can make happen that will bring us luck."

"Gentlemen, follow me, and I will show you the exceptional presidential car."

"Why is it called that?"

"It was built for the company president's use until he became ill. It is the way he traveled in comfort. He had it brought to San Antonio in case he got stronger to use it. He didn't. Sad, sad." Mr. Elgin shook his balding head as he wiped at the perspiration on his face with his silk handkerchief. "Here is the key to unlock the door."

Will accepted the key as he stepped up on the small platform on the side of the car. When he opened the door and walked in, amazement displayed across his handsome countenance. His low whistle was a compliment. The interior was unexpected to a country boy.

Eli likewise was too dumbfounded to say a word. The interior was plush. An elegant crystal chandelier hung over an oak dining table with six red velvet-covered matching chairs, which rested upon an extra thick, brightly colored Persian rug. Velvet drapes as golden as a sunset hung from the windows. More stylish Persian carpets were thrown across shiny oak floors, and a number of dark brown leather chairs were arranged around a smaller marble table.

Along both sides were three compartments, each with gold numbers from one to six on a dark mahogany door to designate the room. Below each number was a solid gold doorknob. Ornate gold hinges glistened in the sunlight.

But the overwhelming focal point of the car took their breaths away. The back of the car was a glass-enclosed sitting area for viewing the countryside. Green velvet couches were attached to the walls. And three gold tables with marble inlays were fastened to the floor to keep them from turning over. The side glasses had rollout levers to open and close the windows for ventilation. No expense had been spared for luxury and convenience.

Mr. Elgin watched in amusement as the two men stared transfixed at the unique and elegant interior of the railcar before he commented, "This is a glass solarium. Very unique for a train, don't you think?"

"Yes, it is. What is behind these doors?" Will asked as he opened the first to reveal a sleeping area. A large bed was fastened snugly to one side, and a marble bedside table was next to the bed with a walkway by the three windows in the compartment; at the other end was a built-in armoire. Each compartment had the same arrangement. Three portal windows provided light and air in each, and for day sleepers, the drapes could be drawn, allowing for privacy.

"Mr. Elgin, we are pleased so far with our purchase. However, we need to find an engineer and crew to run the train. Do you know who to contact?"

"Yes, I do. I will have them come by this afternoon and visit with you. They worked for the previous owner."

"Thank you. Do you know of someone we could get to clean this car today? We are leaving day after tomorrow; we need to be in Fort Worth as soon as possible."

"I will take care of it for you. Good day, gentlemen."

⚊ ⚊

They were pleased with their new toy. But running a railroad would take more knowledge then they had. It would be a learning experience for sure.

When the engineer came by, they agreed to keep the current employees.

The engineer, Rocky Lane, assured them, "I'll start right away on the engine and get the wood box filled to be ready to go. When do you want to leave?"

"We only want the engine and VIP car going. Can you leave the other cars parked on a siding?"

"May I make a suggestion, sir? If you plan to travel to Fort Worth and wait on another train, you will need the dining car to serve food for you, your passengers, and your employees. Also the caboose is needed for your employees to have a place to rest or sleep in."

"Good idea, Rocky; we had not thought of that. Please see to what we will need for the trip and let the others know they will keep their jobs."

"Yes, sir. I'll take care of it. Thank you for the opportunity to work for you. Good day, gentlemen."

As part of the negotiated contract, they would have an express route to Fort Worth to be there in two days instead of the usual three or four days if they had to wait to be sidelined for other trains coming through. It was important to make good time so they could meet Emily Rose's train.

Will and Eli ate dinner in town before saying their good nights as they traveled back to their respective fathers' ranches. At breakfast the next morning, each made the announcement about their plans to take a train to Fort Worth to meet Emily Rose.

"I'm going, too," proclaimed Hannah. "She is my sister, and I'm going to be there when she steps off the train."

"Hannah, you can't travel alone with two men," her mother remarked, scandalized that she would even think about doing such a thing.

Her father readily agreed.

"Oh, Mother and Father, this is almost the 1890s. Don't be so old-fashioned. Times are changing. Besides, I will be traveling with my brother and his brother. How much safer is that? What could possibly happen? A train robbery?"

All eyes turned to Eli, who had sat quietly, watching the shocking turn of events.

"Well, Eli, what do you have to say about it?" Rowdy wanted to know.

"I will leave the decision up to Hannah's parents."

Hannah turned her blazing green eyes on him, silently proclaiming, "Coward!"

"Well, we will talk to Jim to see if Susan wants to go with Will, and if so, you all can chaperone each other. That is the only way we will agree to it," replied Rowdy.

Eli soon left, heading to town to meet Will at the train. Rowdy headed toward Jim's to discuss the matter of their girls traveling with their sons.

"You will not believe what happened this morning when I made our plans known about going to Fort Worth."

"Bet I do. Hannah and Susan will be traveling with us."

"What? How did you know?"

"Same thing happened to me. I got bushwhacked into taking Susan."

"Did you tell them we bought a train?"

"No, did you?"

"No, they think we will be sitting up in a passenger car for three or four days traveling to and from Fort Worth."

"We will make the sleeping arrangements clear in the VIP car. Each girl will have her own room, and when we get Emily Rose, she gets her room. Agreed? Although the idea of having Susan with me is thrilling; it will give us a chance to get better acquainted," stated Eli.

"Hey, that's my sister you are talking about."

"Yes, and Hannah will be there, too. And she's my sister."

"This is a crazy situation you have placed us in."

"Me? You came up with buying the damn train."

"I know. Good idea. Right?"

24

Levi And Emily Rose

Levi was unusually animated at dinner the last night in Pecos. The boarders complimented him on his new appearance and clothes. Was it the new clothes and haircut or something more? Did he want Emily Rose to see him differently from the wounded Indian on the trail?

After dinner, when the kitchen had been cleaned, Emily Rose found Levi sitting on the porch swing in the late-evening stillness. The scents of honeysuckle blooms and lilac bushes entwined themselves in a heady aroma in the evening air.

She sat down beside him as her heart raced at his nearness, and she boldly clasped his hand. "The flowers are truly fragrant tonight, aren't they?" she commented.

Feeling her small, soft hand slide into his large one made him jump. He had not expected her to touch him after their earlier encounter. "It is a beautiful evening now that you are here with me."

Leaning into him, she whispered, "I feel the same way, too. It's nice to sit quietly and enjoy the evening. Tomorrow will begin a very crazy part of this adventure."

"Do you see this as an adventure?"

"Levi, life is an adventure. It is what you make of it. It was an unpleasant experience when it was happening. I was fearful and cried a lot, but I did what I had to do to survive. And am I stronger for having survived it? Yes, I am. And you will be, too, when your memories return."

Levi turned her face to him and kissed her lips. Before the kiss ended, she pressed him for a deeper kiss. And he responded. When she opened her mouth and touched his lips with her tongue, he jerked back, unfamiliar with his own physical reaction to her.

Concerned she had done something wrong, she whispered, "Did you not like what I did?"

Gasping to control his wicked body, he whispered back, "I liked it very much, but we could be getting into a dangerous situation if we are not careful."

Emily Rose smiled as she placed both hands on his attractive face and outlined his manly lips with her long, hot tongue.

Levi moaned as he opened his mouth, sucking in her thrusting tongue. When his began to explore her mouth, she responded with her own moans.

"Emily Rose, I will soon be locking the doors and turning out the lights. It's time to go to your room," called Mrs. Byington sweetly as she moved from the hallway back into the kitchen to lock the back door. This was a respectable boardinghouse, and she did not allow her residents to stay out late. The rule was doors locked and lights out at eight.

Mrs. Byington had succeeded in pouring cold water on the heating couple. Jerking away from Levi, Emily Rose touched her hair and licked her lips, whispering, "I like the taste of you. Good night and sweet dreams for now."

Rising from the swing, she went in, allowing the screen door to slam so Mrs. Byington would know she had come in. She walked up the stairs with a heavy tread so all would know she had gone to her room.

Levi couldn't move. His body was in a rebellion with him. It wanted her badly. He wanted her badly. So badly, in fact, he had resorted to humming hymns under his breath, anything to get his breathing and body reactions under control. His pants had become unusually tight and uncomfortable.

"Levi, are you coming in? I am about to lock the door."

"Yes, Mrs. Byington. I was lingering only to enjoy this lovely evening a little longer." He passed her as he went into his bedroom. "Good night, ma'am."

"Good night, Levi."

After she locked up and turned the lights out, Levi heard her go up the creaky wooden stairs to where she and the female boarders slept.

He walked around his room, gathering his things and packing them into his saddlebags. He had stabled Emily Rose's stolen black stallion and his horse, Powder, in Mrs. Byington's barn, with the understanding that if he did not return and repay her for all she did for them, she could sell the horses to recoup what she had been out. He did not want to lose Powder, but he had no choice at this point. Emily Rose had said life was an adventure. Well, so far he was still on his.

Finally, settling down for the night, Levi undressed, laying his white man's clothes out to wear tomorrow on the train. Riding on a train would be another adventure for him too. He crawled into his white man's bed, pulling the thin sheet over his nude body. Soon his eyes grew weary after he settled his thoughts away from Emily Rose, and he slept.

The rustling of the sheet and the movement of the bed as someone slid next to him brought Levi instantly awake. Emily Rose was here! Her warm, nude body pressed against his back.

Turning to face her, he whispered in the dark room, "What are you doing here? Don't you know not to tempt me like this?"

"I missed you. I wanted to be near you," she said as she wiggled her breasts with their pointy nipples against his chest.

He sucked in his breath and held it. She felt so good against him. His hand automatically grasped one breast and twirled his thumb around the nipple, feeling it harden as he did so. His head reeled from lack of oxygen at what was happening.

"You shouldn't be here. I am barely able to keep myself from loving you. Go back to your room—before it is too late!"

"Do I understand you? You don't want me in your bed?" She sighed as she wiggled more forcefully on his arousal.

"You know I want you. But you don't know what you are asking for."

"But I do. I will leave if you don't want me."

"Oh God, Emily Rose, I want you! But I have nothing to offer you. I don't know who I am or where I come from. I might be an outlaw, for all you know."

"I don't care. I want you. This may be the only night we ever have together, but I will have the memories. Please, Levi, don't make me leave," she whispered as she snuggled closer to his heat.

His resolve...his attempt to do the right thing...his want of her... broke like a bursting dam on a flooding river. He kissed her like a man drowning in floodwaters, reaching—grasping—for something to hold on to.

This time when they kissed, they could not stop the demands of their bodies. He touched her with loving hands, wanting to know every inch of her body.

Emily Rose could not have stopped touching him if she had wanted to, which she didn't. She touched and explored, imprinting the memory of his body and how it felt. They were like two blind people guiding each other in the dark.

When his hot mouth found a raised nipple, she cried out in her joy. He quickly covered her mouth with his hand to stop her from screaming her pleasure and alerting the boardinghouse.

When her hand grasped his hard arousal, he almost lost the control he had been reining in as he tried to wait to make sure she was ready. He liked the feel of her hand. He had never been touched like that by a woman, and the touch sent shocks throughout his body.

She traced his lips again with her tongue, waiting to see his reaction. It was all she could have hoped for. He rolled her on her back and covered her body with his yearning, hard, hot male body.

Wanting all of him, she spread her legs, inviting him in. He rested on her apex as she moved under him, begging in a soft whisper, "Please love me now."

"I don't want to hurt you, darling."

"I am ready."

Without any resistance from her, he touched her to make sure she was ready. As he touched her core, she bucked, wanting him to hurry.

He resisted the urge to hurry, knowing he would hurt her this first time. Gradually pushing in, he made sure she was enjoying the same pleasure he was, even though it was killing him to go slow. She moaned in her pleasure, then gasped when he stopped. He felt the barrier as he pushed farther into her.

She gritted her teeth as her maidenhead tore and she felt the sharp pain, but it did not make her want to stop. She urged him on. She wanted all of him.

His joy rang in his head.

His pleasure rose, but he wasn't sure how to control the timing. It felt so good to be one with her. He was moving in her, and she was moving with him. He felt her excitement growing as he continued to move.

Suddenly, her movements became faster as she bucked and moaned her pleasure saying, "Faster, please faster."

That was all it took for him to lose the control he was holding on his emotions. He rode her long and hard until his seed released deep inside her as she bucked and pitched right along with him. He covered her mouth with his to contain their yells of pleasure at their mating. He had heard stories how people screamed when they climaxed, and now he knew why. It seemed the room was filled with Fourth of July fireworks. The sun, moon, and stars were falling from the sky into their darkened room.

"Oh my God, Emily Rose, are you all right?"

"Oh, Levi, it was more wonderful than I ever could have imagined," she said as she hugged him tightly.

"Then why are you crying?"

"I wanted you so much. And I hope you don't think badly of me. I care for you."

"Oh, darling, I would never think anything but kind and loving thoughts of you. I wanted you, too."

Placing tiny kisses all over his face and lips, she circled his lips with her tongue before sliding it into his mouth. It got the desired response from his lower regions she had hoped. And before long, they were riding the range again before she had to return to her room.

The next morning after a hearty breakfast where they tried desperately to keep their eyes off each other, Mrs. Byington led the way to the train station. She had prepared a picnic basket to travel with them, since they did not know when or where they would have the opportunity to eat.

Approaching the ticket man in the train office, she checked to make sure number 49 was on time. It would be along soon.

Now all they had to do was wait and keep their hands off each other. That had been difficult this morning when Emily Rose had come downstairs with the small satchel Mrs. Byington had purchased for the few dresses she had given her.

Sitting at the same table with Levi and keeping her hungry eyes off him while reaching for bread or butter had been very hard, since she could not help but remember their passion-filled night together. She wanted more!

You hussy, she thought.

It had been equally hard for Levi. Thankfully he had been sitting when she arrived in the dining room or his thoughts would have been visible in the front of his trousers. The best place for his eyes seemed to be on his breakfast plate—definitely not on her.

"Levi, did you hear me?" asked Mrs. Byington.

"I'm sorry. What was your question?"

"Are you packed?"

"Oh, uh, yes, ma'am. I packed before I went to bed last night. Before we leave, I would like to say goodbye to my horse. Will I have time?"

"Yes, we will leave after we clean up the breakfast dishes."

Now they sat on wooden benches in the train station, waiting for the train to take Levi deeper into Texas. He drew in several deep breaths as he contemplated how he had complicated his life by caring for Emily Rose and sleeping with her.

As the train rounded a curve about a mile up the track, its whistle signaled approach. Mrs. Byington cried as she hugged Emily Rose and then Levi.

"Please don't cry. We will see you again," they told her.

"I always cry about everything, but you two have become very special to me. I wish you both the best life has to offer. I know your family will be so happy to have you back in their arms again." She cried more as she wiped her eyes and blew her nose on her embroidered hankie.

The noise of the train was deafening as it roared into the station. Metal wheels screamed in protest when the brakes were applied, and clouds of thick white steam systematically covered everyone on the platform.

Levi had never been this close to an engine before, and his Indian heart nearly jumped out of his chest, making him want to run away. It was all he could do to stand by Emily Rose as she waited for it to stop.

The train conductor opened the passenger car door to allow people off before allowing people onto the train. Motioning for Emily Rose to enter, he helped her step from the platform to the first step on the train. Levi followed after a moment of hesitation. She found them two seats near the front of the car.

After stowing their luggage under their seats, Emily Rose sat down, straightening her skirts. As Levi sat down, she locked arms with him, whispering, "I could hardly wait for us to be alone again. Every time I look at you, I think about last night. Do you?"

"Emily Rose, this is not a good time to mention last night. Too many people are around." But he grinned as he placed his coat over his lap to hide his reaction to last night.

"I wish trains had beds on them. I know where we would be."

"Young lady, I am shocked at your suggestion." Smiling, he wiggled his eyebrows and winked at her.

She giggled and snuggled close as the train pulled out of the station for their long trip to Fort Worth and then home.

25

The Twins

William and Eli agreed to meet in town at eight o'clock with their sisters in tow. They would be bringing them to town in the buggies after saying their goodbyes at the ranches. It seemed like a simple plan, except the girls caused problems with tears and luggage.

Eli argued with Hannah when two ranch hands carried a large trunk to the buggy. It was obviously filled with clothes, and it was heavy.

"No, that is too large for a few days there and back. Don't you have a small satchel like mine to carry your things in?" Eli asked in frustration. "Besides, you always wear pants. Why are you dressed like that today?"

"I'll have you know when I am on the ranch doing ranch work, I wear pants and boots. But today I am traveling to Fort Worth, and I certainly don't want to look like a hick from the backcountry. Now do I?"

"But, Hannah, a huge trunk?"

"Oh, that one is for Emily Rose. Poor girl will want her own clothes when we get her. Mine is on its way down now."

Eli knew when to give up. He had a headstrong sister, and he was losing a battle. He stood back as the ranch hands loaded another heavy trunk into the buggy by the first one.

After Hannah and her family said their goodbyes with tears and waving hankies, Eli slapped the reins on the horse's rump and headed for town at a fast clip, relieved to finally get away.

Will had been experiencing much the same with loading Susan and her luggage. They said their goodbyes, promising to be back as soon as possible.

Arriving at the train station about the same time was a big help, especially since the trunks were large and heavy. Stopping near the sparkling clean engine and VIP car, both girls looked questioningly at their brothers.

"What is this? Don't we need to wait over there for the train to Fort Worth?" Hannah asked as she and Susan were helped down from the buggies.

"We will be traveling in this," Will told her as he presented the new train for her approval. Then gazed with admiration at Hannah in a beautiful green dress instead of pants.

"What? How can that be?" asked Susan as Eli helped her step up into the train car.

"Um, we made arrangements for our big adventure to bring Emily Rose safely and comfortably back home."

"Eli, you sound like Emily Rose when you talk about adventures. She has always been one to enjoy adventures, and I am betting she will have some tales to tell about this one. Our prayers have been for her safety and well-being. We have heard such horrible stories about young girls being kidnapped, and when found and returned, they were never the same." Susan's voice broke as she finished.

Eli patted her hand in a soothing way to let her know he understood.

Taking Hannah by the elbow, Will escorted her over to the steps, attempting to help her up, but she grabbed the handrails to pull herself up, stepping on her skirt and tripping.

"Damn long skirts! I hate them. See, they caused me to fall on the steps."

"Hannah, if you had allowed me to help you, you could have lifted your skirts to find your footing. Here, let me help you up before you tear your dress." Will scowled as he helped her rise and brushed off the front of her dress.

Too embarrassed to comment, she let Will help her enter the railcar. When she stood inside, her reaction was the same as Will's and Eli's had been.

She and Susan stood with gaping mouths, staring at the opulent furnishings that surrounded them. Both turned in a full circle before either uttered a word.

Susan asked, "What is in here?" as she opened the first compartment to discover a fashionable bedroom. "A bedroom on a train? This is too much."

"There are six bedrooms. You may each choose your own suite, and Emily Rose will be in the other. Use this row of bedrooms, and we will be across in the others."

"What is in this one at the front of the car?" inquired Susan.

"We don't know. We never looked." Will, Eli, and Hannah moved to peer over Susan's shoulder at her sharp intake of air.

"It's a necessity room with a bathtub. Oh my, imagine bathing in it as the train is rolling down the tracks." She clapped her hands and squealed her pleasure.

A knock on the forward connecting door had Will calling, "Come in!"

"Mr. Ralston, I am Simpson, your butler and personal valet to assist you while you are on your journey. How may I assist you at this time?"

Will and Eli looked at each other and then back at Simpson. "What do you do?"

"My duties are whatever your needs might require. I serve meals prepared in the dining car by the chef, which may be consumed there or in your private dining area here. I am your valet and will help you dress. I am at your service, sir," he informed them in his perfect English accent as he made a slight bow.

No one moved as each digested what the butler had said. Will regained his voice first. "Simpson, will you help us load the luggage and then let the engineer know we are ready to leave?"

"Yes, sir."

Later the four were seated in the solarium, drinking coffee served from an exquisite china pot with matching cups and saucers as the train shook, rattled, and rocked along the tracks toward Fort Worth. The brothers had never experienced such luxury and knew their half sisters had not, either.

Simpson served lunch at the oak dining table on more exquisite china and shiny, ornate silverware. They could see their astonished faces in the knife blades.

After the noon meal, the girls decided to unpack their dresses and hang them up to shake out the wrinkles. The brothers determined which room they wanted and stowed their few belongings away before returning to the solarium to wait for the girls to finish. It was some time before they returned.

Simpson appeared with refreshments of cheese, crackers, grapes, and a delicious wine for an afternoon snack.

"Simpson, please sit and talk with us awhile. We have questions for you. We know nothing about you, but we did not want to ask in front of the girls."

"Sorry, sir. It is not my place to sit with my employers."

"Very well. Tell us this. What do a butler and valet do? And how did we get you? We didn't know about you."

In his most eloquent English tone, Simpson replied, "I am included in the deal with the VIP car. You see, Mr. Farris, God rest his soul, had this car built and procured me from England to work for him. In essence, I go with the car."

"Do you live on the train? What did you do while it was sidetracked?"

"I live in a small one-room walkup in a not-so-desirable part of San Antonio. To support myself, I have been doing small parties for people who know me and my abilities."

"There are several things we would like to discuss with you regarding your employment with us. First, we do not want the girls to know who owns this train. They are our half sisters, and their families do not know we could buy such an investment. It's a long story. Also, we need you in your quiet way to teach us how to dress, speak, and whatever else you think is appropriate. We were raised on a ranch and didn't have formal training in the better things of life," Will related to him.

"I will be most honored to help you in any way I may." Simpson bowed and took his leave with a smile curling his solemn lips.

"What are you thinking, Will, about Simpson?"

"He seems to be well educated in the things we need to learn to be in the business world. We are on the ride of our lives, little brother, and we need to learn as much as we can about the world we knew nothing about."

Hannah and Susan returned to the solarium, excited about their rooms and delighted to find the refreshments waiting for them.

Susan sat down on the couch near Eli, while Hannah sat with an un-ladylike plop beside Will. They giggled as they sampled the wine in tall, crystal-stemmed glasses.

"Oh, this is good. I have never tasted wine before. Have you, Will?" Hannah asked, flirting over her wineglass at him.

"I have had beer and whiskey, but wine was never an option where we lived."

"Eli, how about you?"

"I haven't been much of a drinker—only beer if we had it."

Susan giggled as she sampled more of the sweet red wine; it rolled smoothly down her throat. The afternoon passed as the two couples laughed and learned more about one another.

Simpson came in to light the gas lamps on the walls and chandelier above the large oaken dining table. The lamps cast a warm glow over the intimate setting.

"Dinner will be served at six," he announced and quickly left the room.

The couples had consumed a number of bottles of wine during the afternoon. It was obvious to a sober person the four were saturated.

Simpson knew from their slurred speech and frequent giggles, he would have to go easy with the dinner wine.

Impressed with the elegant table settings of linen napkins, china, crystal, and sterling silver dinnerware, Will made a toast.

"Here's to good food, good company, and good times," he said as they clinked their glasses together.

Simpson delighted the men with medium-rare steaks with lots of potatoes. The ladies were served with choices of tender prime rib slices, wine sauce, and delicately steamed vegetables.

"Oh, Simpson, how thoughtful of you. This looks delicious," exclaimed Susan as she sampled her vegetables.

Hannah was not impressed with her meal as she eyed the men's steaks, but when she tasted her food, she sang the accolades of Simpson as well.

Eli raised his glass to proclaim, "Our special thanks to the chef for preparing this delicious meal. By the way, what is his name?"

"I will bring him in later to meet you. He was brought here from France to work for Mr. Farris as well. He wanted to prepare for you his specialties in hopes of retaining his position with the new owners."

"Yes, we would like to visit with him soon, and we will pass his wishes on to the new owners. Thank you, Simpson. He is a great asset to our little adventure."

Simpson bowed and returned shortly with more wine. The food had helped to clear their heads of the spirits, and he was thankful for it. He didn't want a car full of drunk and sexually excitable young people.

After the meal was cleared, Simpson asked, "Would anyone care for me to draw his or her bathwater before retiring?"

Taken by surprise, the four young people turned in his direction in unison.

"What? What do you want to do?" Will stammered.

"I am at your disposal if you wish me to draw your bathwater before you retire."

"Uh, uh...no, Simpson, that will be all."

After he left, the brothers and sisters looked from one to the other before breaking out in laughter.

"I was not expecting anyone to start my bath for me." Susan giggled as she hid her rosy cheeks in her hands.

"The thought of a man preparing my bath is so strange to me," remarked Hannah.

"I would do it for you if I could be in the tub with you," Will whispered in Hannah's ear.

"Will, what are you saying?"

"Just that I would do anything you wanted me to do, whether it is for you or with you."

"Is that the wine talking?"

"Hannah, from the first time I looked down into the depths of your green eyes, I have been hooked. Just like you would hook a fish that took your bait."

"That's not quite as romantic as I would like, but it will do. I was caught off guard as well when you spoke to me. I wished I was more presentable instead of being a sweaty cowgirl before a handsome man like you as you towered over me," she whispered back as she touched his handsome face.

Surprised at their admissions to each other, they glanced around to see where Eli and Susan had disappeared to. Together they witnessed Susan's bedroom door closing. And they were left alone in the solarium.

Apprehensive about what that might mean, they looked at each other.

"What should we do about that?" There was concern in Hannah's voice.

"Perhaps they feel the same about each other as we do and they know what they want. Do you?"

"I know they have had several secret rendezvous. But I'm not ready for a leap like that."

"What the hell is a rendezvous?"

"It is a secret meeting between lovers."

"What are you saying about my brother and Susan? They are lovers?"

"Maybe not yet but after tonight, that may not be the case. Don't you know they care for each other?"

Jumping to his feet, he looked down at Hannah with disbelief written all over his face as he said, "Good night, Hannah. Sleep well."

He crossed the railcar to his bedroom, where he spent a sleepless night tossing and turning with thoughts of Hannah alone in her bed just across the way—and what Eli and Susan were doing in her room.

The next morning, Simpson waited until they rang for him before entering the VIP car. It was already midmorning when he took the china tea service filled with coffee because he knew the barbarians in this country drank the vile liquid. He much preferred the civilized drink of hot tea. He shuddered at the thought of coffee. Setting the service on the dining table, he served the four as they quietly sat on the couches in the solarium. He noticed the lack of twangy Texas talk from the girls and the quiet of the plainspoken men.

"Chef Pierre will prepare your breakfast as soon as you are ready. Please let me know what you would like prepared."

Receiving a silent nod from Will, he departed.

The silence hung like ghosts in a graveyard.

Will was blurry-eyed from lack of sleep; Hannah's eyes appeared puffed and swollen from crying. Eli and Susan were equally silent. The only sounds in the car were the clickety-clacks of the metal wheels on the tracks, periodic engine whistles, and the ever-present rocking from side to side as the train moved rapidly toward their destination.

Everyone jumped when Will asked, "Well, what would you like for breakfast? There are omelets, waffles, or biscuits and gravy."

When Simpson returned, he took their requests and returned to the chef. Before long he was back, carrying the delicious food along with heavenly smells of the hot, freshly baked bread.

As they ate, the mood changed back into the fun times. Susan asked Simpson what the previous owners had done on long trips.

He replied, "There are a number of things available to pass the time. If one prefers to read, there is a small library behind the doors near the butler's pantry. Also, there are a number of card games or checkers in the drawer below the library."

"Thank you, Simpson. You are most helpful."

During the day, the train made several water stops to fill the boiler in the engine, and one long stop to replenish the wood car. At those times, the two couples left the railcar and walked around outside to stretch their legs and get relief from the constant rocking motion of the train.

"It is so hot today. I'm glad there are trees at this stop, unlike the earlier one," remarked Susan as she walked arm in arm with Eli.

When they had moved farther away from Eli and Susan, Will apologized for the way he had acted. "Hannah, I am sorry about last night. I didn't intend for it to end like that."

"I'm not sure what I said that upset you, Will."

"I suppose it was the fact my brother had not said anything to me about his feelings for Susan. But I realized I had not discussed my feelings for you with him, either."

Shocked but pleased, Hannah stared at Will before she found her voice. "You have feelings for me?"

"I have since the moment you climbed down off that bronco you were breaking and looked up at me. I have wanted to take care of you."

Taking Will's arm, she whispered to him, "Will, I have never been one of those girls who likes fancy clothes and big parties. I am very different from my cousin Susan. I wear pants and work on a ranch. I'm not ladylike like she is, if that is the kind of woman you are looking for. It's not me."

"Hannah, my mother wore pants more days of her life than she wore dresses. She was a horse rancher, and when we were growing up, she did most of the work herself until we got big enough to help. I am a simple man, but I do want to become better educated. Most of my life has been spent on a ranch. I am discovering there is a different world out there than the one I was raised in."

"Will, I have feelings for you as well. I hope they will continue to grow. I like what I see of the man you are. I have always loved Uncle Jim. Did you know his wife, Rachael, and my mother, Ruth, are sisters? They came to Texas after the war and met Father and Jim. I see so much in you that I have loved in Uncle Jim. He has always been a good husband and wonderful father to his children."

The train whistle interrupted their conversation, and they turned in the direction of the VIP car. Will and Hannah were the last to board. Will whispered in Hannah's ear, "Maybe tonight we could try out the bathtub."

Hannah's face turned bright red, as she whispered back, "Let's don't get carried away too soon, I don't want to rush our feelings. OK?"

Will's loud laughter caused Eli and Susan to look back and see Hannah's rosy red cheeks. Deciding not to comment, they moved on to settle in the solarium as the train began to move.

26

Levi And Emily Rose

The final day of their train ride to Fort Worth dawned quietly. Levi had been sleeping with his head resting in his left hand. When he jerked awake from a dream, his hand and arm were numb. It was a terrible feeling. Shaking and moving them caused him to jar Emily Rose awake.

They were both exhausted and weary from lack of sleep and hurry-up meals when the train did stop long enough. When the engine needed water and wood, it stopped in designated areas along the way. Levi, Emily Rose, and other travelers would take the opportunity to walk around the train in order to get exercise and find the necessity room provided for the passengers, but very few stops offered food. And most stops did not last long.

According to the conductor, they were expected to be in Fort Worth by six tonight, barring any problems.

"Will we get off this train and on to the one going to San Antonio?"

"There will be the six-thirty p.m. leaving for San Antonio tonight or the seven-oh-five tomorrow morning." After answering her question, the conductor continued through the cars, announcing to the weary passengers a longer-than-usual stop for breakfast.

Emily Rose looked at Levi as she said, "Well, it doesn't leave much time to eat before we have to leave again. I wish I had gotten more money from Mrs. Byington so we could stay over tonight and catch the train in the morning. I am so hungry and weary."

"I'm sorry, honey; I know you are tired. But we will manage somehow. I had a strange dream. I dreamed I was flying like a bird. Actually, it was a black hawk. I could feel the wind on my feathers and the up and down drafts of the currents as I circled. Then a mighty eagle joined me. When it turned its head, it had my father's face."

"What do you suppose it means, Levi?"

"I don't know, but I had no fear of the eagle. I also sensed I had flown before. A sharp pain like a bullet ripped into my heart, and I began to spiral downward. I saw the trees, the ground, and sharp rocks coming toward me. Before I hit, I jerked awake."

"Oh, Levi, how terrifying. Do you think it has a meaning, or was it just a dream?"

"I knew it was my father, and that was comforting. I had a feeling from him that all would be well. So...I will dwell on it as a good omen, although I am not sure what the ending of the dream could mean. Was it a warning I would be shot and this time die? Or did it have a more prophetic meaning, like I would suffer heartache?"

Emily Rose gasped at his last comment as if it had pierced her heart as well. Soon she would have to tell him she was the one who shot him, causing his memory loss, but she was afraid of losing him. Her feelings for this wonderful man had grown stronger with each passing day, and she did not want to lose him because of what she had done.

"No, let's think it is a sign from your father that all will be well. The train is stopping. Let's have breakfast before we have to continue with this dreadful train ride."

After they stepped down from the car, Levi presented her with his arm, and he escorted his lady into the depot restaurant.

After breakfast, they had time to clean up and change into cleaner clothes for the rest of the trip. Before boarding, they purchased bread and cheese for a light lunch. Refreshed after the stop, they climbed aboard lighthearted and ready to see what the day held for them.

Late in the evening, three whistle blasts signaled the train entering the Fort Worth station. The weary travelers gave a loud shout of cheer as their long trip across Texas came to an end.

Emily Rose sighed loudly as she remarked, "We will depart this train and climb onboard another. Not a happy thought, is it?"

Levi patted her arm that was entwined in his. "As long as we are together, it makes the trip less dreary, my darling."

"You make me happy, Levi. When you meet my family, please don't let them overwhelm you. You will always be welcome there."

"Thank you. But this adventure, as you call it, has opened my eyes to how people respond to Indians and the rejection I personally experienced. Although I knew how the white man has treated my people with the killings and taking of their lands, this journey has placed me in a position to learn firsthand what they have experienced. I was ignorant of it. The white man has expected us to know our place, but what place is that? Many questions! Traveling with you when I am dressed as a white man has not presented any rejection situations."

"I can't promise you others won't treat you badly, but my family will not. Oh, look, we are coming into the station. Hope we don't have trouble finding the right train. The station is so large."

As the engineer threw the lever for reverse, the squeaking brakes screamed their protest, and steam bellowed out from the engine wheels as the train rolled to a stop.

Emily Rose and Levi were the first passengers to be allowed off. When she stepped down onto the platform, the steam cleared momentarily, revealing her sister, Hannah, and cousin, Susan, standing there.

Screams filled the air as the three girls rushed toward one another. Their jubilant reunion full of ear-piercing shrieks, joyous crying, and embracing took place as passengers getting off or getting on the train moved about them.

"What are you doing here? How did you get here?" cried Emily Rose as she hugged them both.

"Oh, Emily Rose, so much has happened since you were taken. I don't know where to start. We each have a new brother we did not know anything about until they came looking for our fathers."

"I have another brother? When? How?"

Susan finally controlled her crying long enough to say, "They are older than us and belong to another mother, but they are so like our fathers. Here—I want you to meet them." She turned to look for Will and Eli.

But the brothers were no longer watching the tearful women. They were staring at an unexpected figure emerging from the fog of steam.

"Black Hawk? Is that you? Why is your hair cut short, and why are you dressed like that? What are you doing here?" stammered Will.

Levi turned toward the familiar voice standing behind the women. "You know me?"

Will and Eli exchanged glances before surrounding him in warm embraces, certain it was Black Hawk who was dressed as they had never seen him before.

"Yes, we know you. You are our brother, Black Hawk. What are you doing here in Texas?"

"I...uh...don't know...who I am or why I'm here."

"Levi, you are here with me to meet my family. Don't you remember?" Emily Rose called to him.

At the sound of her voice, Levi turned toward her and then looked back at his brothers. His face became a slate of emotions as the dark vale was split open to reveal his memories of who he was and what he was. He looked from one to the other in confusion. His memories rushed in—happiness, good times, family, grief, deep sadness, loneliness, hurt... deep emotional upsets, and profound physical pain.

Turning toward Emily Rose, he pointed his finger at her as he shouted with hate-filled anger. "You are the one who shot me! I remember seeing you aim the rifle and shoot me. Why did you do it and lie to me about it? Why?"

Grabbing his chest, he passed out from holding his breath at the shock of his revelations. His brothers caught him in their arms as he collapsed.

27

Levi

Distant sounds of the busy train yard could be heard through the open windows. A slight breeze blew the scents of woodsmoke, oil, and dust as Black Hawk struggled to rise to consciousness. A heavy weight was lying on his chest, making his breathing difficult.

A voice in his mind was saying something to him.

"Remember the vision of the black river where the Council of Ancients talked to you? Your destiny has been foretold, but only you have the power to accept it. It will not be forced upon you. You have experienced only a small taste of what our people have suffered at the hands of the white man. It is your destiny to make it different. You must see with your heart what is to be done in order to forgive and make it better."

Black Hawk's memories flooded him again as he felt a tender lick across his face as if he had been kissed. Opening his eyes, he gazed into the sky-blue eyes of Silver, his mother's wolf. Too surprised to react at seeing him here, wherever here was, he raised his hand to stroke the silver fur. When his hand touched the soft fur, Silver disappeared.

Why should anything surprise a tribal medicine man that is familiar with the spirit world? It was comforting to know he was being guided to seek out his destiny. As he continued to think about all that had happened to him, he became aware of voices from the other room. Hearing Emily Rose speak made his heart jump for joy, but then he remembered her betrayal.

"I was so afraid of being followed when I escaped the Apaches, since I had taken the leader's black stallion. I traveled for two days without food except a few pieces of jerky because I was afraid to shoot the rifle for fear they would be close enough to hear it. I had crossed a mountain stream and sat down to rest. I heard sounds of hooves and was terrified they had found me. I raised the rifle and shot as soon as the Indian came around the boulder." She cried harder as she remembered the terrible feeling of killing a person.

"When I saw there was only one Indian, I hid in the bushes to make sure he was alone. Then I slipped over to see if he was dead. There was a large silver wolf standing over him. It began to pull items from his waist pouch. Later I realized it was medicines to doctor his wounds. Is that not strange? I was thankful he wasn't one of the Apaches. I took care of him as best as I could under the circumstances. I was glad I had not killed him, but he lost his memories of who he was. I couldn't leave him alone like that, so I brought him with me. You know the rest," she wailed. "And now he hates me, and I love him so much."

Hannah pulled her sister into her arms, soothing her. "Now, Emily Rose, it will all be fine. You need to give him time to work everything out. He is as confused as you are with this strange situation."

"Yes, who could have ever guessed we would come to Texas to find our fathers and find our brother here, too. It gives me the shivers to think of all the weird things happening to us," remarked Eli as he thought of his visions. "I have not told Will about my last vision of Black Hawk."

All eyes turned to stare at him.

"Another vision, little brother?" asked Will.

"Yes, I dreamed I was flying as a hawk, and soon an eagle joined me as I circled. When the eagle looked at me, it had the face of Eagle Talon.

Suddenly, I had a piercing pain in my chest, like an arrow had been shot into me, and I was spiraling to the ground. I jerked awake before I hit."

A scream from Emily Rose startled everyone. "Levi...uh...Black Hawk had the same dream this morning when we were on the train. What does all this mean? I am so afraid and confused."

"Until he wakes up, we will not know. But let's have our dinner and some wine, and I know we will feel better then," declared Will.

"Levi and I have not had much to eat today. I am very weary and hungry. Dinner sounds wonderful."

After ringing for Simpson to prepare the table, Will directed the girls to show Emily Rose to her room and help her to settle in. He motioned for Eli to follow him and went into Black Hawk's compartment.

Discovering Black Hawk was awake, the brothers greeted him with, "Welcome back. You fainted and have been out for a while. How do you feel?"

"Like I have been trampled by a herd of buffalo and didn't die. Where the hell am I?"

"You are in Fort Worth, Texas."

"I know that much. But what is all this?" he asked as he waved a hand in the air.

"Oh, this. Eli and I had a big plan to buy tickets on a train to Fort Worth to meet Emily Rose and ended up buying a railroad," Will said proudly.

"How could you afford to buy something like this?"

"Did you not read Mother's journals and then talk with Mr. Miller?"

"Yes, Raven and I both did."

"Raven is back at the ranch?" asked Eli, surprise in his voice.

"Yes, she is, and that's another story but back to this one. You bought a railroad. So what will you do with it?" asked a bewildered Black Hawk as information whirled in his brain.

"We decided it would be a good investment with all the money Mother has provided for us. So we each paid half and are now partners in a business."

"Do you know how to run a railroad?"

Will laughed. "No, but we are willing to learn, and what better place than in Texas after we get these girls back home."

"Did you see Silver just now?"

"No, but we have both been seeing him at unexpected times. And how did he get to Texas?"

"Don't you both get it? He is a spiritual being. He can be anywhere. He was here to remind me about my journey to my destiny."

"Wow, Black Hawk you are really starting to sound like you need more rest," replied Eli as he looked around the room.

"You both know Father was a powerful spiritual medicine man. He had an eagle spirit guide. He named me Black Hawk because I also have a spirit guide, which is a black hawk. It allows me to soar in the sky just as Father could fly as an eagle."

"OK, you are really scaring me now. You believe you can fly? Do we need to get a doctor to look at you?" whispered Eli as he looked from Black Hawk to Will.

"Eli, what Black Hawk is trying to tell us is he has the same powers as Eagle Talon. We know this to be true, but we have chosen to ignore it because we have not experienced it. Not until this trip, which has been like a lightning rod to me. Hasn't it been so for you?"

Eli did not reply.

Will continued. "Black Hawk, I have come to understand myself more since we have been on this journey. I have found a father I never knew existed. I have grown closer to my twin brother, and I have begun to understand you as the special person you are because of your powers. Mother's journals have set all of us on our own journeys to seek out our own destinies."

"OK, I want to know what and how you found me. How did you know I would be here? I knew you both had come to Texas to look for your fathers. But here? I am truly confused. Will you please explain?"

Before either could utter another word, Simpson announced dinner was served.

"We will continue our conversation later. You need to eat and gain strength now that we are all together," Will told Black Hawk as he helped him rise from the bed. Together he and Eli escorted their brother to the elegantly dressed table.

Black Hawk was thunderstruck to sit at such a table with fine linens, china, crystal glasses, and ornate silverware. He did not protest when Will seated Emily Rose next to him.

"Black Hawk, this is Simpson, our knowledgeable butler, who will serve us a wonderful meal prepared by our chef, Pierre."

"Master Black Hawk, it is a pleasure to meet you," announced Simpson in his most British voice.

"It is my pleasure to meet you as well, Simpson." Black Hawk looked from him to his brothers with a questioning glance.

Will stood up as he said, "Let's raise our glasses to a successful trip to escort Emily Rose safely back home and to the discovery of our brother, Black Hawk."

The clinking of the crystal glasses and crying of "cheers" were heard as they began their first meal together.

28

Emily Rose And Black Hawk

After dinner, the siblings talked for hours about the circumstances that brought them to Texas and what they might do in the future with the knowledge they were gaining each day. Emily Rose and Black Hawk told everyone about their difficult journey to Pecos and Mrs. Byington, who had helped them.

Growing weary from the long, emotional day, Emily Rose announced, "I am taking a bath in that wonderful tub with lots of hot water and going to bed, where I will probably sleep for a week. Wake me up when we get to San Antonio. Good night, everyone."

The group broke up and went to their separate sleeping quarters as Emily Rose went into the bathing room and closed the door behind her.

She had removed her clothes and was running water in the oversize tub, smiling as she dreamed of sinking into its watery pleasures, when a soft knock sounded at the door.

Holding her robe up before her, she quietly opened the door, smiling broadly when she saw Black Hawk grinning at her.

"May I come in? I need to talk to you," he whispered to her.

Stepping back so he could come in, she held up her robe, covering her front, but that was about all it was covering.

"You should not be in here. My sister may hear you."

"I wanted you to know how I regret my reaction earlier today. I can't describe how it hurt me to know you shot me, but I now understand the whole story and why. Will you forgive me for what I said?"

Tears welled up in Emily Rose's eyes as she looked at the man she loved. "I have worried about what would happen when you found out, but I hoped by that time you would love me as much as I love you. I wanted to tell you myself. I didn't know you saw me shoot you. I am sorry for hurting you."

Black Hawk stepped closer, taking her into his arms as he kissed her sweet lips and tasted the wine she had enjoyed.

When she raised her arms to encircle his neck, her robe was forgotten as it slipped to the floor.

The moment they touched each other a charge shot through them as if a bolt of lightning had found them in a closed room. Nothing else mattered but the two of them. Nothing else mattered but having each other. Nothing else mattered but...

"Oh my goodness, I forgot about the water, Black Hawk. Quick... Turn it off."

Rushing over, he turned it off before the water splashed over the top. "We better let some out before you get in, or it will run over." He laughed as he reached down to open the drain, getting his sleeve wet as he did so.

"Will you stay and bathe with me?"

Surprised that she had voiced what he was thinking, he turned to look at her in all her shapely glory. It was almost his undoing.

"You are so beautiful. I have never seen a woman without clothes."

"Not any of the village maidens?"

"No. I have never bathed with a woman before," he stammered.

"And do you think I have ever bathed with a man?"

"No, of course not. But..."

"But what?"

"Our brothers and sisters are here. What would they think if they knew we had slept together and were now bathing together?"

"Can you not see our brothers and sisters have taken a liking to each other as well?"

Black Hawk looked at her and then at the door.

Emily Rose wasn't sure if he was thinking about bolting out the door or locking it, but she knew what his decision was when he took his clothes off.

Stepping into the warm water, she sighed her pleasure as she sat down and reclined on the sloped tub. Smiling up at him as he stripped, she said, "Your body is beautiful to me. I like looking at you."

He didn't need a second invitation before he stepped into the bathwater with a silly grin on his face.

"Do you like what you see?"

"Yes, I do. I remembered how you felt in the dark, but nothing can be more exciting than seeing you in the light." She giggled as she made room for him.

She handed him the scented soap, and he lathered his large hands and slid them over her body.

"Oh, Levi...er...Black Hawk...what am I supposed to call you?"

"I don't care as long as you will love me like this always." When he pulled her on top of him in the full-length tub, the sensation of their wet, naked bodies sliding together was heavenly.

"Oh, darling, doesn't that feel good? I like you wriggling on top of me. Now slide down on me...Yes, just like that...Aaww. I can die just like this."

"Hmm, I like you just like this, too."

A knock at the door stopped them instantly.

"Emily Rose, are you all right? Were you calling me?" asked Hannah as she waited for the lie. She had heard a male voice as well as Emily Rose's giggles.

"No, I'm fine, uh...just singing. Good night, Hannah."

"Good night, Em. Sweet dreams."

"Oh, I will have sweet dreams tonight."

Hannah looked into Black Hawk's bedroom, knowing he was not there. She then moved silently to the next room and knocked softly on Will's door. He opened it with a grin and took her hand, leading her inside as he closed the door.

"Do you know what Black Hawk and Emily Rose are doing? They are bathing together. I don't know what to do about it," she moaned.

"Hannah, we talked about doing the same thing. They just beat us to it," Will reminded her.

Shocked at his comment, she protested, "But...but...what will our parents think?"

"Uh...who is going to tell them?"

"Oh, right. But what if they find out?"

"Then we will deal with it at the time. Now why did you come to my room alone late tonight? Did you want something from me? I know I want something from you."

He laughed softly when he saw the realization of his meaning dawn on Hannah. Pulling her into his arms, he nuzzled her neck, kissing her ear as he continued his upward rise to her mouth.

"Oh, Will, yes...yes..." She sighed as she kissed him back. Groaning, she pushed him away. "No, Will. Please don't tempt me. I must go. Good night," she said as she went back to her bed and a sleepless night.

The next morning, Simpson served the three couples their breakfasts at the dining table. As he withdrew from the room, Black Hawk tapped on his water glass to get everyone's attention.

"I have something I would like to say to our little group before we go any further into this day. I want to talk about what has brought us to this point in time. I do not want any misunderstandings between Emily Rose and her family."

"First, I am a Ute shaman, like my father. I was on a vision quest to find a certain place in New Mexico. At the Valley of Fires, the Great Council of Ancients visited me and explained my destiny would be revealed. It was exciting and confusing, but I knew it would be shown to me in due time—whereupon, I crossed the path of Miss Emily Rose, and you know the rest of that story."

The siblings laughed.

"Do you mean we were meant for us to meet there?" Emily Rose asked with surprise as she looked at the others.

"Yes, it was meant to be. I know now what I need to do to help my people. It may take me looking like a white man to get it done. I am asking each of you to help me in any way you can to accomplish this."

"Black Hawk, you know you have Eli's and my full support to help your people, whom we love just as much as you."

"Thank you. I experienced firsthand what my people have endured for a long time. I see what my destiny is now, and I must learn and grow to make it happen.

"My Ute grandmother, a powerful medicine woman, has taught me many things. I will not give up the old ways, but I will seek different paths to find how to help all tribes."

Simpson entered the car. "Mr. Ralston, are you ready to leave for San Antonio? If so, I will notify Mr. Lane."

"Yes, please do so."

29

The Brothers

The return trip to San Antonio seemed to go quicker than the earlier one. Happiness reigned onboard the VIP railcar.

As the siblings arrived at the Rocky Mountain Ranch, both families and many of their friends were waiting to greet Emily Rose on her safe return. There were few dry eyes at the joyful reunion. A barbeque and dance had been planned for Saturday to continue the celebration. To show their support to one of their own, a large group of Texas Rangers had escorted Emily Rose and her family back to their ranch.

The families were surprised when Will and Eli introduced their brother, Black Hawk, who had met up with Emily Rose in New Mexico. Captain Jones shook Black Hawk's hand, remarking, "I'm glad you survived the shot in the head."

At Black Hawk's surprised look, Captain Jones explained, "I had made Texas Rangers out of your brothers, and we were traveling to the Mexico border, searching for Emily Rose, when Eli had a vision of you getting shot, and it scared them and my other fierce Texas Rangers to death. We had to return to San Antonio."

"My brothers are Texas Rangers?"

"Not anymore. When they refused to continue to the border, they resigned. Eli also told me to stay away from that place. It is a very lawless place, full of outlaws."

Black Hawk's eyes glazed over as he looked at Captain Jones. In a strange voice, he said, "Yes, death waits there for you."

Captain Jones's reaction was of anger as he said before walking away from Black Hawk, "A lawman's death is always facing him."

Jim pulled Will aside, asking, "Did your mother have anything to do with all this?"

Laughing at the question, Will said, "I have no idea except to say that according to Black Hawk, Emily Rose is part of his destiny."

Later in the day, the brothers returned to San Antonio to the Menger Hotel. They wanted to impress Black Hawk with their accommodations. It beat the hell out of sleeping on the ground.

Black Hawk was duly impressed as he was led into the sophisticated hotel and up to the suite of rooms. Before going up, they had inquired if it was possible to have a three-bedroom suite.

Shortly after they entered their suite, service help arrived to move them to a larger suite. Following the men, the brothers were amazed to be taken to the penthouse floor. Larger and more spacious rooms were spread out before them.

"Wow! I thought we had beautiful rooms before, but this has surpassed that. What do you think, Black Hawk?"

"I am speechless. I had no idea people lived like this."

"Hey, come over here and look out the windows at the tiny people below. Look, here is a porch we can walk out on," Will pointed out.

"Excuse me, sir. It is a balcony," clarified Simpson.

The brothers were startled to hear his voice and turned in unison to stare at him.

"What are you doing here?" asked Will.

"Sir, I am your butler and valet and travel wherever you go. I arranged for the additional room accommodations after I heard you tell Black Hawk he would be staying here with you. I hope you are pleased with the penthouse. If not, I can make additional changes for something less grandiose."

"No! Grandiose is fine. I mean, we like how you think, Simpson. I am sorry I did not realize you could take care of things like this. Remind us if you see things that need to be done."

Eli stepped forward, asking, "Where will you stay, Simpson?"

"Thank you for asking, but the penthouse accommodates hired help who travel with their employers. Chef Pierre will be coming from the train, with your permission, to prepare your meals in the kitchen here, and I will be available as well with a ring of a bell."

"After we settle in, we need to have a meeting to make decisions about what we plan to do about our futures. OK?"

They agreed as they all went in different directions to their rooms.

Hours later, after much discussion, the brothers decided to learn how to run a railroad and assist Black Hawk in helping his people, and all were in agreement about remaining in San Antonio to be near the girls.

"Speaking of the girls, I need to ask each of you a personal question about your relationships with them," stated Will.

No one said anything, staring at him.

"Since I am the oldest, I think I need to ask the first question. Eli, you and Susan spent time alone in her compartment on the train. I am concerned something may have happened to cause problems with Jim."

"Oh, that. It is none of your business, but I will tell you because I do not want Susan's reputation to be in question. We took the time to be alone to talk about how we felt about each other and if we could grow to love each other. There was a little kissing, but that was all. What about you and my sister, Hannah? I don't want trouble with Rowdy because you took advantage of her."

Will laughed before he replied. "Me take advantage of Hannah? She's a rough and tough Texas gal who can hold her own. We, like you, have only managed time alone to become better acquainted and see if anything could grow from our feelings."

"OK, I understand," said Eli.

When only silence came from Black Hawk, all eyes turned toward him.

"Why are you so quiet? It makes me nervous when you are so quiet," Stated Will.

Black Hawk stood up, walked over to the windows, and stared out, remaining silent as he gathered his thoughts.

The silence was deafening.

"Emily Rose and I have grown to love each other. I think I knew that from the moment I opened my eyes and she was there. She took my breath away. She is beautiful with a big heart that cares for nature and people. I do not want anyone to think badly of her because we were alone together. But they will anyway because of the outlaws and then the Apaches. It is human nature to think the worst."

He cleared his throat before continuing. "We will marry soon."

"Thank you for sharing with us. I am hoping Hannah and I will continue to grow closer as well," replied Will.

— ~ —

Early the next morning, when Simpson served breakfast in the elegant dining room, he casually mentioned he should accompany them to the clothier district to purchase clothing required by their new lifestyle.

"Why should I wear fancy clothes, Simpson? I don't want to appear to look down on my people," asked Black Hawk.

"But, sir, you will be dealing with white people who need to look up to you and want to please you. If you do not meet *their* standards, they will not let you in the front door, and you will not gain the help you need."

Black Hawk stared at Simpson a long time before he spoke.

"You are a very wise man, and I appreciate your counsel in this matter. You are right about how people perceive me. It does determine how they react to me. I am reminded of how I felt in Pecos when I was shunned because I was an Indian or half-breed. No one would help us because of it."

"OK, Simpson, how soon do you want to take us on to teach us how to dress?" Will laughed.

"It might be easier for all concerned if I take one at a time, so I can concentrate on the individual and his needs. Who would like to volunteer to be first to become a proper gentleman?"

No one raised his hand.

"All right, I chose you, Mr. Will, to be first. When do you want to go?"

"Uh...how about after we finish breakfast?"

"Please pull the large tapestry hanging in the corner when you are ready to go." He bowed and left the room.

"Wow! You will come back a perfect gentleman." His brothers snickered.

"Aww, but you two are next," hooted Will.

Hours later, Will and Simpson returned with a barrage of people carrying boxes loaded with boots, shoes, different styles of hats, suits of every color, and all the accessories that went with a properly dressed businessman.

Will collapsed in a brown leather chair as he waved Simpson and the entourage toward his bedroom. "You can handle it from here, Simpson."

"Did you buy out the stores?"

"Not every one. Ha! We managed to visit most of them, though. And at each one, we caused a stir when Simpson made known what we wanted. I did succeed in acquiring Texan-made shirts and a new type of working pants called blue jeans. They are made from a denim fabric and are becoming popular with ranchers. Be sure and get you several pair. You will like the way they feel. See, I managed to wear them here without Simpson yanking them off me," he said as he stood up to model the new Texas fashion.

After lunch, Eli was the next one to venture out with Simpson. Each had to make the trek around the city with Simpson to acquire new clothes.

⁓ ⁓

The next day, Will and Eli dressed in their new business clothes and visited the owners and operators of the other railroad lines coming into

San Antonio. It didn't take them long to discover all were having finan-cial problems and could be persuaded to sell.

They were directed to an accountant, a Mr. Jennings, who could explain how railroads made their money and all the problems involved with running a railroad business.

"Mr. Jennings, I am Will Ralston, and this is my brother, Eli. We recently purchased a small railroad and need your advice as to how to get it up and running. We have been sent to you because you have a good name and know how to make money in this business."

"Thank you, Mr. Ralston, for your consideration. I will do my best to work with you. Tell me, what are your plans with the new line?"

"My brother and I purchased the line on a whim and are hoping we do not live to regret it. We need to learn the business and want to make money in this venture. What do you suggest our first step in accomplish-ing that be?"

The conversation continued for several hours. When Will and Eli left, their heads were spinning, but they knew more about how and what they wanted to do with the new venture. They were learning.

While his brothers went in one direction, Black Hawk dressed in his "white man's clothes" and visited the government office of Indian Affairs.

What he discovered made him heartsick. It was plain to see the gov-ernment and its bureau of Indian Affairs considered Indians scum and forced them into treaties to relinquish their lands. The treaties lasted about as long as it took for the ink to dry, then more demands were made on the Indian tribes. The government's desire was to rid the world of Native Americans and their way of life living off Mother Earth and to assimilate them into American society.

When Black Hawk returned to the penthouse, he sat the rest of the day, staring forlornly out the windows. Sorrow filled his mind and heart at the atrocities committed against Native Americans. His thoughts pro-duced an array of emotions from concern to deep despair.

When he remembered his vision with the Ancients, he sank further into the depths of self-loathing because he could not do what was expected of him.

Simpson appeared silently by his side. "May I get you something to eat or drink, Master Black Hawk?"

"I wish to be left alone, Simpson," was his surly reply.

Hours later, his brothers found him sitting on the balcony, still in deep sorrow.

"What has happened to you? Are you sick?" asked a concerned Will.

Eli rushed over to feel his forehead to see if he had a fever. His hand was slapped away.

Black Hawk remained silent.

"Has someone died? Please tell us what is wrong."

"What is wrong cannot be fixed. What is wrong has gone on for a long time, and nothing I can do will ever be enough to fix it," whispered Black Hawk.

Both brothers knelt down beside his chair, grabbing his arms to sooth him.

"We are here for you. But we can't help if we don't know what has you so upset. Tell us."

"I have lived in my own little world, isolated in the mountains all my life. I did not know what was happening to Indian tribes in other parts of the country. I knew my tribe was having problems with whites as they invaded more of our hunting grounds, but I turned a blind eye to their troubles. Today I discovered the extent of the hatred the government and white people have for my people and what they have done to the fierce warriors, women, and children by killing and driving them from the land the Great Spirit gave to them." Black Hawk lowered his head and shed tears of great sadness for his People.

Only the sounds of the street below could be heard as the brothers held one another, sharing the excessive sorrow together.

"What can we do?" asked Will as he wiped tears from his own eyes.

"I have learned the government passed a law several years ago called the General Allotment Act. It will take more lands from the Native

Americans, forcing them to live on reservations, to give up their religious beliefs, and to try to become farmers, taking them from the life the Great Spirit taught them. They are being assimilated into modern society to remove them from the ways of the Ancients. I don't know what to do."

"We must hire lawyers and find people who know how to fight the government through the courts. You have told us about your vision with the Ancients. They chose you because you can understand both sides of the problem. We know you can do this. You are discouraged now because of what you have learned today, but you will use it to help all the people, Black Hawk. We know how strong you are."

Looking up through blurry eyes at his brothers, Black Hawk was encouraged to know they were there to help him.

"You are right to remind me tomorrow is another day, and I need to prepare myself to fight for my people. I will choose to fight for Native Americans as I walk the path as a white man." Laughing, he continued. "And I pray I can be the one to make a difference in their lives."

Eli looked proudly at Black Hawk. "We both know you have the ability from Mother and Father to be strong. Now let's eat. I'm starving."

"You are always thinking about your stomach." Black Hawk laughed as Will rang for Simpson.

During dinner, Will remarked, "I am really missing Hannah. I am thinking I may propose to her tomorrow night at the barbeque."

Gasps came from the others at the table. "I have been having the same thoughts about Susan. I stopped today and looked at a hacienda that is for sale. I wondered if she would like a home like that," Eli said.

"What if the girls turn us down?" asked Black Hawk.

"Well, the only way to know will be to ask. Right? I think I may visit a store I saw today that sells wedding rings. Anybody want to go with me?" asked Will.

The dining room chairs scraped as the brothers quickly left together to promote the next step in their futures.

30

The Party

A ctivity at the Rocky Mountain Ranch was at an all-time high. Ranch hands started early, cleaning the barn and building a dance floor for later that night. Under the ancient Live Oaks, barrels and large wooden planks created tables to hold the mountains of food that would be coming when the neighbors arrived. In Texas you didn't go visiting without bringing food. Already the morning air was filled with delicious aromas of food as the women prepared bread, pies, and cakes for the feasting tonight.

Several large pits were dug, piled high with mesquite wood, and ignited. When the fire burned down to coals, sides of beef would be added on spits to sputter and sizzle as they cooked for the barbeque tonight. The ranch cook and his sons worked to prepare a special barbeque sauce he created to mop on the beeves, adding to the flavorful smell scenting the air.

Another large fire pit was burning under an enormous cauldron filled with pinto beans, which had soaked overnight.

Ruth would soon be adding small pieces of salt pork, powdered chili pepper, jalapeños, and onions to flavor the beans.

Rowdy was overseeing the ranch hands with the help of his young sons. Ruth was directing the extra help in the kitchen, and Emily Rose and Hannah were cleaning the house as everyone prepared for the big celebration.

Will and Black Hawk rode up just as the girls were dragging large rugs outside on the porch to beat the dust out of them. After jumping down from their horses, they raced up the steps to help the girls with the heavy load.

"We are happy to see you," flirted Emily Rose as she brushed up against Black Hawk. "We wondered if we would ever see you two again."

"We have been busy. You know you can't get rid of me that easily, Emily Rose," he said as he pushed her to the wall and kissed her hungrily on the lips.

A sigh escaped her as her passion flared.

"Uh, will you two cut that out! Someone might see you," yelled Hannah as she motioned Will to come around on the side porch, where she waited for her kiss. He was happy to oblige her.

"Where is Eli?" asked Emily Rose as she looked around for the other brother.

"He rode over to see Susan. He wanted to bring her with him when he came over. Anyway, we are here to help. What can we do?"

"After we finish beating these rugs, would you like to walk down to the river, Hannah? I need to talk with you." Will smiled as he looked passionately at Hannah.

Hannah hurried through the rug beating, excited to have time alone with Will to see what might come up.

— ~ —

At that moment, Eli was riding up to the Forever Ranch house. He was looking for Susan, but he hoped to have a chance to visit with Jim for a while.

As luck would have it, Jim was sitting on the front porch, enjoying the cool morning breeze before it turned steamy hot by noon. He shouted a greeting to Eli. "Hi, son. Come on up and sit with me."

"Good morning, sir. How is your leg progressing?"

"It is doing very well since Will fed me to the maggots." Jim laughed heartily at his joke. "Between the maggots and the Indian herbs, I have continued to gain my strength as it heals. What brings you here so early today?"

Eli dropped his head and looked at his shaking hands before he was able to say anything.

"I...uh...wanted to talk to you and ask if I might court Susan, and if she is willing, I would like to ask for her hand in marriage," he croaked out.

A horse whinnied down at the barn corral, the wind whistled through the mesquite tree branches, and the purple sage brushes danced along the fence. Jim said nothing, only stared straight ahead.

Eli cleared his throat, asking, "Sir, did you hear me?"

In a whisper, Jim replied, "Yes, I heard you."

Again, silence hung between the two men.

"I had thought this moment would be a long time in coming and Rachael would be here to share it with me. Do you realize how strange this is for me? You are Rowdy's son by Laura, and you want to marry my daughter by Rachael."

"Yes, sir, it is overwhelming what has happened to me the last three months to bring me to this point. When spring began in the mountains, I did not think I would be anywhere but there. Now here I am in Texas, meeting a man I never knew existed and wanting to marry a beautiful woman...if you will allow it...and she will have me."

Again came a long pause as each considered the situation and how strangely it had come about.

Eli rubbed the back of his neck as he hunched over the chair arms before he spoke again. "Since I have come here, strange things have been happening to me, such as having the visions and seeing Silver. I am not sure if it was a one-time happening or if they will continue, if that is your hesitation about accepting my pursuit of Susan's hand."

Jim had remained silent as he listened to Eli. He asked, "What do you have to offer my daughter? Will you work as a ranch hand on my ranch or someone else's? I want more for her than that."

"Sir, Mother set up trusts for each of her children. Through wise investments, she grew the trusts into financial strengths down through the years. I discovered recently I am a wealthy man. I had expected to raise spotted horses on our mountain ranch, but Mother had planned otherwise. I can support Susan in a fashionable way. I have looked at homes in and around San Antonio because I would like to be able to keep her near her family, but I also will travel to my ranch near Denver as well. I want your blessings on our union."

"So you have already worked this out, have you? Have you spoken to Susan about any of this?" he asked as he raised a questioning brow at Eli.

"Not exactly. I know she cares for me, as I care very deeply for her."

"Susan, I know you have been listening at the window. Come out here. I want to know if you love this man."

Jim and Eli heard her gasp as her father called her name.

Susan appeared on the porch, blushing at being caught eavesdropping.

"I know you heard most of our conversation. This man is asking to court you and expecting to marry you. What say you about that?"

"Father, Eli and I have had a connection from the moment we met. It has only grown stronger. I would be honored to have him court me," Susan told her father as she lowered her head, unable to look at either man. Her thoughts danced to the time of the train ride, when the two had learned more about each other.

"I wish your mother was here to enjoy this moment," Jim remarked in a low whisper.

"I know, Father. I do, too. I miss her every day and am sad she is not here to know Eli as we do. She would love him, too," Susan said as she wiped tears with her sleeve.

"Well, if you are agreeable to Eli courting you, I will give my blessing. I do hope you will stay around here for a long time and help me raise this wild bunch I have on my hands," he said as he laughed good-heartedly.

Eli jumped up, grabbing Susan, swinging her around on the porch. They had much to talk about now that Jim had given them his blessing and the first step was out of the way.

31

Rangers And Outlaws

Captain Jones and the other Texas Rangers had been busy as well. Word had come down from other lawmen that Blackjack Ketchum was back in Texas. Rumors were spreading he was still gunning for the two Rangers he had thought had been killed in the Easter raid.

The Rangers were planning to attend the celebration at Rowdy's tonight, but they would rotate the men in and out of the party so Rowdy, Jim, and the other partygoers would not be aware they were guarding the perimeter.

When Blackjack found out the raiders had captured Rowdy's daughter, then traded her to Indians, he had been livid. They had no way of knowing who she was because she pretended to be a crazy girl, and they were afraid of her. He had killed the men for the botched ambush, weeks later discovering the truth. He searched for the redhead, but she had disappeared. Upon finding the Apaches who had her, he was angry to learn she had poisoned them and escaped. He wanted to harm her to get back at Rowdy and the other Rangers. But fate was against him.

Excitement ran high as the party got underway. Wagons and buggies filled with friends began to arrive, followed by cowboys on horseback, anxious to join the celebration.

The women and young girls were helped from the wagons and pulled out red-and-white-checkered cloths to cover the makeshift tables. Bowls of potato salad, Mexican rice, enchiladas, hot tamales, empanadas, and flour and corn tortillas, along with platters piled high with fried chicken, baked bread, and every kind of pie, cake, and cookies known to man appeared on the tables. When the eating started, gallons of hot sauce would flow like the beer from the five kegs the men had set up near the barn.

A large cowbell drew everyone's attention as Rowdy and Ruth motioned for silence.

"Ruth and I want to express our thankfulness for your prayers for our Emily Rose's safe return. We praise God for her safety during the horrific events of Easter Sunday. Let us pray for Jim and his family as well after the loss of Rachael to such a meaningless act from those who sought revenge. Thank you all for coming. After the pastor gives the blessing, we will eat and celebrate this joyous occasion. Pastor Everly, if you please."

Following the blessing, the eating began. Huge platters of barbequed beef had been carved and set on the end of the table with all the other meats. Delicious food smells to tempt everyone. Beer flowed from the kegs as well. The party grew louder with the high pitch of women voices overshadowing the low treble of male tones, yells from the children as they chased one another, an occasional baby's cry, then the music makers started to tune up their instruments for the first dance, adding to the crescendo. Happy sounds of merry making surrounded the partygoers.

— ~

Earlier in the afternoon, Will and Hannah had walked hand in hand down to the San Antonio River. In the shade of the huge Live oaks, he pulled her into his arms and kissed her sweetly on her lips. The kiss intensified until Hannah had to pull back, sensing Will wanted more from her than she was ready to give.

Moving away from him, she whispered, "Will, I am concerned where this might lead. You have expressed your desire to become a railroad owner and live in the city. I'm not sure I would be happy there."

"I would like to know how you truly feel about me. The other is only location. I thought you had begun to want me in the way I wanted you."

"I do care for you, and I am drawn to you as if we belong together, but I want to know you better."

"I understand your hesitation. I know I am rushing you, and I don't want you to feel that way. I want our feelings to grow toward each other."

Hannah wandered over to a fallen log and sat down as she said, "Will, I didn't know you existed until recently. It has been a strange revelation to all of us. I have feelings for you. I want my feelings to grow to be sure they are real. Do you understand what I am trying to say?"

"Yes, Hannah, I understand. But I am prepared to do whatever I need to do to win your love. I wanted to talk with your father today about courting you with the intention of marrying you. Are you agreeable to me talking to your father?"

Hannah looked up at him in a different way as a smile appeared on her lips, and a rosy glow pinked her cheeks. "I would like that very much. I may be a tomboy and break wild horses, but I am still a woman at heart and will be thrilled to be courted."

Will pulled her to her feet as he encircled her in his arms. He said, "I know I have rushed you the last week, but I care for you. I will do everything to make you happy and take care of you as well."

Before he could say any more, Hannah placed her hand on the back of his neck, pulling his head down to her waiting lips. His lips brushed over hers before she encouraged him to deepen the kiss. As she opened her mouth slightly, Will drew back as he looked down at her, waiting for his kiss. Her eyes were half-closed as she looked up into his through her lashes. He softly placed angel kisses around her mouth before thoroughly kissing her as he pulled her tightly to his heating body.

The kiss left both breathless, and Will whispered in her ear, "We must go back before I do something shameless like rub myself on you like this."

Hannah giggled as she rubbed his arousal, which was pressing between her legs, as she whispered back, "Yes, we better not do that to each other."

When they broke apart, Hannah straightened her dress and smiled at Will as they walked hand in hand back to the activities of the day. Will planned to look for an opportune time to talk with Rowdy, hoping his reaction would be a good one.

As they returned, Hannah was called into the kitchen to help with the food preparation, and Will joined Black Hawk at the barn as he and the other men got acquainted, sampling the beer as another keg was tapped.

After a light lunch of sandwiches under the cooling shade of the live oaks, a respite from the growing heat, they all returned to their chores for the celebration.

Will and Black Hawk had an eye on Rowdy as he went down to the barn to check on a mare that was in foal. They followed, hoping to have a private conversation with him.

Rowdy stopped at the back stall, watching the mare for a few minutes as Will and Black Hawk circled him on each side.

"Well, boys, it looks like she is definitely in labor. I hope it happens before the noise of the party gets into full swing. I don't want to upset her."

"Do you think we should move her to a quieter location?" asked Will.

"No, I want her here where I can watch her. She lost her last foal because she got into trouble, and I want her near enough this time to help. Nearly lost her as well."

"We understand, sir. On our ranch, we let nature handle it, but if there's trouble, we step in. We will be happy to help you any way we can," related Black Hawk.

"Thank you. I will call on you if she needs help."

"Uh, sir, Black Hawk and I would like to have a quiet conversation with you, maybe out back here away from the ranch hands."

Rowdy's eyebrows shot up as concern creased his forehead. "Sure, come on out here so we can talk by the back corrals."

They followed Rowdy through the back door until he turned suddenly in their path and said, "Well, what is so serious we need to come out here?"

"Well...sir...I...uh...we..." stammered Will.

"Sir, I want to ask your permission to court Emily Rose and marry her by the fall. I hope you and Mrs. Adams do not have any problems with me being half Indian," declared Black Hawk proudly.

Rowdy and Will gawked at Black Hawk.

Silence filled the space except for the cussing of the ranch hands as they worked and talked about their problems, the whistle of the hot wind blowing through the barn, and the soft sounds of labor coming from the mare.

Rowdy cleared his throat as he watched Black Hawk sweat.

"Well, I don't know much about you except what has been said about how you and Emily Rose met. I would like to know more before I can make a decision. Just because your mother was Laura doesn't necessarily make this situation right, but it doesn't make it wrong, either. Many people in Texas have suffered much at the hands of Indians. I know feelings run high, and I don't want my daughter to be subjected to being shunned because of you."

"I have never known what it was like to be shunned, as you called it, until I arrived in Pecos. I was made to feel I was worthless and a piece of garbage. Since I have been in San Antonio, I have dressed like a white man and used the name my mother gave me, Levi. People have treated me differently. I am amazed how the way you dress and the color of your skin make people react differently to you."

"I am at a loss for words to that, but I know it to be true. However, I do not want my daughter, if she accepts your suit, to ever have to live in an Indian village or reservation."

"Let me assure you now. Emily Rose is the love of my life, and I will do everything within my power to keep her safe. Our mother left her children wealthy from investments and trusts she set up years ago for us. But I do want you to know I am on a mission to save the Native Americans from the government and anyone who wants to destroy them. Will I be found in favor with everyone? I am sure not, but as I grow in knowledge, I hope to be able to do what needs to be done."

"Surprisingly, you have impressed me with your dedication to your people. Are you planning on running for Congress to put your best foot forward to get it done?"

Black Hawk stared at his future father-in-law a long time before he finally spoke.

"Mr. Adams, you may have been the cog in my wheel that I needed to truly make a difference for Native Americans. Perhaps that will be a starting place to get me to Washington. What do you both think of that?"

Will had remained quiet as he listened to his brother, who usually was quiet and slow to express himself. He'd done it quite well this time. Now he was thinking about running for Congress! Perhaps this would prove to be the way for him to fulfill his destiny.

"I am amazed you would consider such an undertaking, for I know your heart bleeds for your people. I say bravo, Black Hawk," answered Will proudly as he patted his little brother on the back.

Rowdy nodded in agreement.

"Now, Will, what did you have on your mind? Am I to lose another daughter?"

"No, sir. You will not be losing either. But we are hoping you and Mrs. Adams will be agreeable to gaining two new sons-in-law in the near future. Hannah is reluctant to agree to marry me, but she will. She has said she would be pleased to let me court her, if you will allow me to do so."

"Will, I know very little about you, either. Tell me what your plans are for the future."

"As you know, until recently we three brothers lived in the Colorado Mountains on the Spotted Horse Ranch. We never expected any more from life than to live out our lives doing what we had always done. And that was work. With the death of Mother and the shock her journals caused, we have been in a whirlwind of emotions. We never dreamed we would travel to Texas to discover our fathers, find new families, and discover the loves of our lives. Eli and I have already made some investments and are looking to make more. We want to stay in or around San Antonio because from what we have seen, it is becoming a business center, and we want to be a part of it. With the money we have, we can pretty much do what we want to. We want to stay close to the friends and families here. Since I grew up on a ranch, I am interested in purchasing ranch land along the rivers in the area."

Again, Rowdy was silent as he digested what both men had told him. Finally, he answered them.

"I understand your bewilderment. As a young, single man, I never thought about the consequences of what my actions might be because I loved Laura. As I find out more about destinies from Black Hawk, I am reminded constantly that our actions do matter. I have come to know you were brought here for a purpose by a greater power than me. So who am I to forbid you from courting my daughters? However, they are almost of age to be allowed to make their own choices of whom to love. I appreciate the information about yourselves. Good luck in wooing my daughters. You will both need it. You will have your hands full. Believe me," he said as he laughed, good-naturedly shaking their hands.

32

Outlaws And Rangers

Everyone who attended the gala was happy for Emily Rose and her safe return—except for the outlaws who were crawling on their bellies in the dark to surprise the guests and shoot the two hated Rangers and any members of their families who got in their way.

Blackjack Ketchum had insisted his gang of outlaws do the job right this time. The imbeciles who'd botched the job before had not had a plan except to ride in and start shooting. His plan was simple. He wanted a massacre at Rowdy's ranch this time—something no one would ever forget.

He observed the festivities from high on a hill with the army binoculars he had taken off a dead army officer. As the hour grew late, the men's movements become sluggish from their beer consumption, and the women grew weary from their many duties throughout the day. He signaled his second in command, who would lead the raid.

Earlier he had ordered, "Billy, take the men now and surround the party. When you get closer, have the men lie down and crawl on their bellies the rest of the way. I want them to shoot everyone, but make sure you kill the Rangers first. I want to get them this time. Do you understand? There is so much noise from the music and boot stomping on the dance floor you will not be heard, but do go as quietly as possible. I want to watch their faces when the surprise raid starts. I will wait for you here. Go!"

Billy and the large gang of outlaws rode down the hill to where they were to leave the horses and slither like snakes through the underbrush.

An occasional gasp or muttered curse was heard as the outlaws became entangled in briar vines, as sharp mesquite thorns jabbed into their arms and legs, as several brushed against sharp prickly pear cactus thorns, and as one scared voice yelled out he had been bitten by a snake. Another found a polecat that sprayed him. He yelped as he ran back toward the horses. The thick smell of skunk drifted over the area.

The dancers turned in the direction of the faint breeze scented with skunk as they covered their noses, probably thinking one of the ranch dogs had stirred up a polecat.

Mothers had rounded up their young children, placing them in the backs of their wagons on mats to sleep for the journey home tonight. Food was covered, and empty platters and bowls had been cleaned off the tables and put away as the dancing began.

Many of the men who were not dancing were keeping the beer kegs working as suds spilled into many glass mugs. The party was in full swing, and everyone was having a wonderful time, unaware of the impending doom.

Rowdy and Ruth stepped up on the dance floor as the music ended. He tapped his knife against his beer mug to draw everyone's attention.

"Ruth and I have an announcement we want to share with our friends and family. Levi has asked for Emily Rose's hand in marriage. And she said yes. Emily Rose is engaged to marry Levi Ralston. We will let you know when the wedding will take place, and everyone is invited."

A loud cheer went up as beer mugs and tea glasses were raised to honor the happy couple that stepped up on the dance floor beside Emily Rose's parents.

Billy was in position now and had a clear shot at Rowdy when he began to speak. He looked for Jim, seeing him standing to the left of

Rowdy. As he took his deadly aim for Rowdy's heart, a boot came down on his gun hand, and a gun hammer clicked as it was cocked next to his head.

"If I was you, I would say my prayers, dickhead. You are under arrest," whispered Captain Jones.

"Who are you? What are you doing here?"

"The Texas Rangers always take care of their own, and we figured that son of a bitch, Blackjack Ketchum, would plan something like this. Now get up and start walking back to your horse."

A grumbling Billy joined his men as more Rangers emerged with outlaws from the underbrush.

"Where is Blackjack?" asked Captain Jones.

"He is watching from up on the hill. He wanted to see it happen and enjoy every bit of it."

Captain Jones signaled his men to tie up the outlaws as he and two others mounted horses and rode up into the hills.

As the late-night moon rose, it created a silvery glow on all the trees, bushes, and trails. They searched but were unable to find Blackjack before he slipped away.

Captain Jones decided Blackjack had waited for the shooting to begin, and when it didn't, he knew something had gone wrong with his bloody plans. Disappointed to miss apprehending him, Captain Jones returned to the other rangers and Blackjack's gang. At least he had them to hang.

The Rangers had to listen to the one who was snakebit moan all the way back to town and the one who stank of polecat was tied on his horse and brought up the rear. But the powerful smell still was overwhelming when the wind blew in their direction.

— ⁓

The celebration continued, as the guests were unaware of the near fatal attack. As it grew late and the moon rose higher, casting its bright light, the dancing and drinking dwindled, and the partygoers started to load their wagons to head home.

Good nights were said as the last wagon and riders left. Black Hawk hugged Emily Rose as he nuzzled her neck and whispered sweet words of love to her.

She hugged him tight, not wanting this night to end, but she had to let him go, since his brothers were saying their good nights to Hannah and Susan. She did not want him to travel back to San Antonio alone.

They watched as the two couples parted and went in different directions to have their time alone as well.

"I wonder if your brothers are in love like we are?"

"From what I can tell, they are. But Hannah has Will worried she does not love him like he loves her."

"I know Susan and Eli are very serious about each other. She has talked to me about how she grows to love him more each day. Hannah has not talked about her feelings. She likes to be her father's tomboy, but I think she will soon learn how much she loves Will. I think she wants to take her time and be certain he is the one."

"Do you have any concerns about my love for you?"

"No, I don't. I knew from the moment I saw you I could care for you, even when you were lying bleeding at my feet. I prayed you would not die without knowing how much I cared."

"My goodness, Em, that's quite a statement. How could you know then?"

Emily Rose smiled lovingly at him as she pulled him close. "Destiny."

Black Hawk laughed, as he had shown her she was his destiny as well.

"I have many questions I want to ask you about what we will do, but I will save them for another time. I am excited about planning a fall wedding. Are you?"

"Emily Rose, I have never planned a wedding, nor do I know the first thing about it. I know I want us to marry as soon as we can because I can't keep my hands off you. But we do have your father's blessings and are now engaged. I pray I can make you happy with our life together."

The depth of his feelings for Emily Rose astounded Black Hawk. His lips sought hers, but she suddenly gave a startled cry when she saw a movement under the shadow of the large live oak tree.

When Black Hawk turned to look at the shadow, it moved into the moonlight toward the couple.

Words formed in Black Hawk's mind as he heard Silver's voice saying, "You have done well, Black Hawk. Your chosen mate will be a comfort for you, as you will be for her. You will be happy, but your path will be rocky as you work to help your people. Go in peace, my son."

Silver's sky-blue eyes shone brightly at the loving couple before he turned and disappeared into the shadows.

"Did you see that? That is the strange wolf I saw standing over you when you were shot in the mountains. And several more times before you woke up."

"Darling, did you hear what he had to say?"

"Oh, now you are talking to wolves?"

"He came to let me know I have chosen well for a mate. As wife of a shaman, you must become accustomed to strange happenings. I hope you can understand and not be afraid. My love will keep you safe."

"Oh, Levi, the fun we will have with all the spiritual beings that follow you. I will always love Black Hawk."

They walked under the ancient Live oak tree, and the shadows covered them as they snuggled in each other's arms.

THE END

About The Author

Augusta began to put her characters down on paper when the muses in her head tormented her until she let them tell their stories. Her stories are fiction, but the men and women she writes about are real to her. She uses light humor and "plays on words" to make the reader think about the meanings of the passages. She remembers the fairy tales of her childhood, which always ended with "happily ever after." But she soon learned in real life, it doesn't always happen that way. Augusta hopes her writing will inspire women to take control of their lives and make a better world for themselves and others.

Augusta lives in the beautiful Texas Hill Country with her family, assorted dogs and cats, and feeds native whitetail deer outside her yard fence. She is an avid birdwatcher and loves most of God's creatures, except spiders and snakes.

Augusta would love for you to follow her on Twitter—@Runawaywriter—and Facebook, and to purchase any of her books, go to her website, Augustawright.com.

Embrace the Journey

Augusta Wright

www.ingramcontent.com/pod-product-compliance
Lightning Source LLC
Chambersburg PA
CBHW060108260626
47160CB00005B/1831